Radio-Terror

Radio-Terror

by
Eugène Thébault

translated by
Fletcher Pratt

A Black Coat Press Book

Acknowledgements: I should like to thank Georges T. Dodds for providing valuable materials and Paul Wessels for his generous and extensive help in the final preparation of this text.

Introduction Copyright © 2011 by Jean-Marc Lofficier.
Cover illustration Copyright © 2011 by Yoz.
Inside illustrations by Frank R. Paul.

Visit our website at www.blackcoatpress.com

Introduction

Eugène Thébault's *Radio-Terreur, Grand roman du Mystère*, translated here as *Radio-Terror*, was initially published in a serialized version in the magazine *L'Aventure* Nos. 1-30 in 1927-29, then reedited and collected by publisher Arthème Fayard in 1930. It was that version that had the honor of being one of the very few French works selected by Hugo Gernsback to be translated by none other than Fletcher Pratt, the well-known author of *The Well of the Unicorn*, and it was published in the June, August and October, 1933 issues of *Wonder Stories*.[1]

Eugène Thébault was born in 1864 in Arthenay, a small village in the Charente region in Western France. He died in Viroflay, near Paris, in abject poverty, on January 5, 1942.

Thébault was a journalist and a prolific popular novelist, who made his debut in 1894. He collaborated with a wide range of newspapers and magazine including *L'Écho de Paris, L'Aurore, Le Matin, La Petite République*, and *La Revue de Paris*. He was a renowned art critic from 1896 to 1906. As a novelist, he penned many thrillers and romance novels, such as *Mademoiselle Midinette, Sauvé par l'Amour* [Saved by Love] and *Les*

---

[1] For *Wonder Stories*, Pratt also translated S. S. Held's *La Mort du Fer* (1931) (as *The Death of Iron*), *Wonder Stories*, Sept., Oct., Nov. & Dec. 1932) and Charles de Richter's *La Menace Invisible* (1934) (as *The Fall of the Eiffel Tower*), *Wonder Stories*, Sept., Oct. & Nov. 1934.

Chevaliers de la Croix Noire [The Knights of the Black Cross].

In 1909, under the pseudonym of "Paul Zahori," he wrote a Holmesian pastiche, *Mademoiselle Sherlock*, which was first serialized in *Le Figaro*, and later collected in book form by publisher Tallandier and released in their imprint "*Le Livre National*" (No. 840, 1932). In it, an 18 year-old Parisian woman, obsessed by Sherlock Holmes, becomes a detective herself.

Thébault also used the nom-de-plume of "Amaury Kainval" to pen a series of popular detective novels for Ferenczi: *En Plein Mystère* [Complete Mystery] (190?), *La Bande des Foulards Verts* [The Gang of the Green Scarves] (191?) and *La Mort dans l'Ombre* [Death in the Shadows] (1919), *La Nuit Rouge* [Red Night] (1920), *Le Cachet Magic* [The Magic Seal] (1921), On Frappe dans l'Ombre [They Strike in Shadows] (1922), *Le Piège Infernal* [The Infernal Trap] (192?).

Finally, Thébault also wrote several science fiction novels, including *Radio-Terreur*. The ones we know about are:

* *Le Magicien de l'Air* [Wizard of the Air] (19??), serialized in *La Depêche de Toulouse* but not collected in book form,

* *L'Aile Invisible* [The Invisible Wing] (1918), serialized in *Le Journal*, also not collected,

* *Le Surhomme* [The Superman] (1927-28), also written under the nom-de-plume of "Paul Zahori," never collected in book form.

* *Nina, Australe Mystérieuse* [Nina, The Mysterious Austral Creature] (1930), initially published by Gedalge, but reprinted by Tallandier in 1932 in their "*Grandes Aventures*" imprint under the better known title of *Les Deux Reines du Pôle Sud* [The Two Queens

of the South Pole]. This novel about the descendents of an ancient Babylonian civilization living secretly in the Antarctic and gifted with powers between science and sorcery was considered a masterpiece by science fiction scholar Pierre Versins, who devoted two pages of his Encyclopédie to its review.

* *Le Soleil Ensorcelé* [The Spellbound Sun] (1930), also reprinted by Tallandier in *"Grandes Aventures"* in 1933.

The information contained in this brief introduction was mostly taken from a recent reprint by the magazine *Le Rocambole* (No. 7) of *"La Mort du Mage"* [The Death of a Magus], a short story which Thébault dedicated to Camille Flammarion, dealing with communication with Mars, which was published in *Paris-Journal* No. 33, November 7, 1908.

Jean-Marc Lofficier

With the immense panorama of the empty Place de la Concorde spread before them, Mazeller suddenly gripped his assistant by the arm. To the flamboyant red of the skyline there succeeded an orange light.

CHAPTER ONE
THE FIRST BROADCAST

On October 18, 193*, the weather in Paris was marvelous, and numerous groups lingered along the boulevards in the early afternoon to yield themselves lazily to the caresses of autumn.

At the Place de l'Opéra a great crowd had gathered before the perfected loudspeaker which had just been installed there for the benefit of the public. Its powerful voice dominated the clamors of the traffic which rolled unceasingly past like a triumphal parade.

The loudspeaker, with a clarity and tone that delighted the assembled public, was reproducing the sounds of a cleverly assembled concert in which eight educated dogs, three elephants and a dozen parrots were performing a rendition of Beethoven's *Ninth Symphony*. The eight dogs were in London; the three elephants were in Calcutta, where one of them was tooting a trombone, the second a bassoon, and the third an oboe especially constructed far this gigantic and rather unusual performer. The dozen parrots sang (if one could call it that) from Buenos Aires; and everything had been arranged by the world radio commission so that all the different members of this extraordinary choir could be heard by wireless enthusiasts in any part of the universe.

As a matter of fact, the reception was all one could hope for. The elephant oboe player had just finished a solo, executed with deafening virtuosity, when all at once the thread of the animal concert was broken, to be replaced by an absolutely insupportable sound of frying.

"Well!" remarked someone, "what's going on? I don't seem to be able to understand the words anymore."

People laughed, imagining that the disagreeable sounds were part of the program.

A blonde *midinette*,[2] declared gaily:

"I know what it is; they've tuned in on some pigs asking for their soup."

"It's extraordinarily well imitated," affirmed a young radio enthusiast in a tone of conviction.

Suddenly, the sound of frying ceased, and after a few seconds of incomprehensible silence, a voice came from the loudspeaker, a sharp, dry, tearing voice, but so clear that every syllable enunciated was heard.

"*Listen!*" said the voice. "*Listen! The world is coming to an end!*"

A burst of laughter greeted this announcement. The first speaker cried:

"Is that all?"

A serious-looking gentleman shrugged his shoulders. "Wait. A new publicity trick," he explained.

But the voice in the loudspeaker began anew, trembling with vibrations of hate and anger:

"*Listen! I, whom you do not know and who hate and despise all of you, announce that I have found a method of annihilating mankind and destroying the world! Listen! In an hour the world will be destroyed! In an hour, do you hear? Nothing will exist anymore, neither you nor the Earth that supports you! I am the master of unknown forces and of waves possessing an infinite power of destruction. I am the master, the only master of the universe! And I desire that the universe shall perish.*"

---

[2] A Parisian salesgirl. (Ed.)

The only result of this emphatic speech was to raise an even greater hilarity.

"Too bad," shouted the joker, "that I didn't know about it three days ago. It would have saved me paying my rent."

A tall young man who was tranquilly lighting a cigarette chipped in:

"—And with me getting married next week!"

And the *midinette* added:

"The radio's a bore today—just when the animal concert was going so well, too! Somebody ought to call up about it."

The general opinion seemed to be that some practical joker was amusing himself at the expense of the crowd. But the crowd did not go away; everyone waited for the words that would show what the clever speaker was advertising. The cloudless sky held an autumn sun so warm that everyone felt amused and indulgent; at certain times of year it takes very little to please Parisians. The loudspeaker began again:

"*I hate humanity and I have condemned it. All human beings are criminals; they injure themselves, they kill each other, they deserve to be punished. I, who speak to you, I, against whom you can do nothing, I, who can do everything, am going to precipitate all of you back into the nothingness from which you should never have emerged! I am going to give you a proof of my power. You see what time it is? Look at your watches; in ten minutes the Sun will disappear; the shadows will cover the whole Earth and become thicker and thicker; no light at all will be able to shine in the night that I create...*

"*Listen! Listen! In 20 minutes a glacial cold will replace the present warmth. Your limbs will be para-*

lyzed and then you will begin to believe what I tell you. I hate you, all of you, you living people, who, in an instant, will be nothing but so many corpses. Your bodies will not fall to dust—they will be annihilated! Have you never thought what it would be like—not to exist? Well, you have 50 minutes to prepare yourselves for it."

A frightful laugh, amplified by the loudspeaker, sent a tremor through the crowd. The voice continued:

"*I hate you. I wish your agony could last for centuries. But in 50 minutes no living thing will exist anymore.*"

The voice fell silent; a silence filled almost with agony. But the clear laughter of the *midinette* dissipated the general sensation of terror.

"I have it!" she said. "It's an ad for a fur company! If it weren't so warm, I'd take my 30,000 francs and buy me a moleskin."

The serious gentleman added:

"The joke is in bad taste. Why don't the police do something about it?"

Nevertheless he pulled out his watch and glanced at it, an action imitated by the major portion of the hearers of this unlikely discourse. Then, as though in spite of himself, he looked at the sky.

Not a cloud! The benevolent Sun shone down on them, reassuring and magnificent. Decidedly, the *midinette*'s idea was the most likely explanation of this unexpected and ultra-modern method of getting people's attention.

All the same, in this crowd which remained so skeptical and so little moved, there was one person who seemed to take this incredible announcement hurled on the ether, apparently by some melancholy joker, at its face value. It was a young man of some 22 years, who wore the smock and cap of a Parisian laborer. His thin, serious face bore an expression of the keenest attention, as making play with his elbows, he worked as close as possible to the loudspeaker and waited to hear it again. But no one paid any attention to the growing surprise and fright that spread over his visage.

The Place de l'Opéra was black with people, and hurrying crowds of the curious overflowed down the boulevards, filling the Rue de la Paix as far as the Place Vendôme, flowing down the Rue Auber and into the Rue du Quatre-Septembre, growing larger every second through all the streets where one could hear the voice of the loudspeaker. The clever merchandiser who had thought of this scheme to advertise his wares, had certainly attained his object. He must have been a clever psychologist to thus play on idle dolts with a display of superior doltery.

Meanwhile, a good many of the strollers, thinking the show was over and that the interrupted concert would hardly be resumed, began to go their separate ways when the loudspeaker began again.

"*Watch!*" clamored the gigantic voice, "*watch the Sun! It is going to darken, and in two minutes the cold will begin.*"

At these words, the young workman made desperate efforts to get away. He succeeded in escaping from the crowd, got around the Opera House, and raced as fast as his legs would carry him down the Rue Auber. It was time; there was a terrible surge among the mass of people and cries of fright rose from all sides. A sinister shadow, like that of an eclipse, spread rapidly from west to east, hiding the Sun and then spreading rapidly across the heavens to plunge the whole city into a nightmare dream. And in every direction, propagated by terror with the speed of an electric current, the news that a frightful and inevitable catastrophe was upon the world spread through the city, invading every district, racing down every darkened street.

In the sudden obscurity there was the wildest disorder. As the voice had predicted, it was impossible to light either electricity or gas; and in the crisis produced by this abnormal night, no one thought of taking steps to insure order and quiet movement—not that any such steps would have been of the slightest use.

In that wild crowd of men and women who had suddenly become the prey of an inexpressible horror, nobody had the cool-headedness even to think of the supernatural individual who had boasted of being able to destroy the world and who seemed in a fair way to do it. Everyone thought of the horror; no one of its author.

Was the unknown really going to realize his terrible prediction? And in destroying the Earth and all its living beings, would he not destroy himself as well? Was the same thing happening all over the world as in Paris? So many problems, so many questions—and no one able to answer them, all were incapable of intelligent thought. The movement in the streets and boulevards was completely halted, an agonized silence weighed down the crowd, as everyone heard only the oppressed breathing of his neighbor.

Suddenly cries of despair broke forth, heart-rending appeals, wails, shouts of rage and the dumb sound of blows, revealing the combats for life the dark concealed. It was for anyone who could to make his way through the crowd by main strength, to find his way through the opaque black toward his home, there to exchange a last farewell with his family before plunging into nothingness. The prediction was being realized; a brief and final agony was beginning for the human species, brief, but so terrible that seconds seemed to last for centuries.

Once more the voice of the loudspeaker rose above the crowd, sarcastic and insulting:

"*Everything I promised you is really going to happen... Now prepare for the cold! The polar cold, which you would not be able to resist even if I should renounce the joy of destroying the Earth and all its inhabitants. In a few minutes, in 30 minutes at most, there will be no more people alive.*"

And in fact it was as though an icy blanket fell suddenly upon Paris. Then, after a few seconds the cold was accentuated, it became so bitter that no one among the victims of the diabolic unknown had even the strength to shiver. In an absolute silence, like that of the tomb, in a night as profound as that of the sepulcher, the loudspeaker counted the last moments of the world, before it should be re-absorbed in the infinite,

"*Still ten minutes more!...Five minutes more!*"

Near the loudspeaker a single soft voice rose in a sobbing plea:

"My God!"

As though the prayer had been heard, the enemy of the world cried from the loudspeaker:

"*Two minutes more—and the world will be destroyed.*"

CHAPTER II
THE HELIUM LAMP

At the exact moment when the crowd in the Place de l'Opéra was finding itself much amused by the concert of the dogs, the elephants and the parrots organized by the three amusement trusts of London, Calcutta and Buenos Aires, the engineer Gribal was preparing to leave his little apartment on the Rue Boissy-d'Anglas. His wife, daughter and son were meanwhile listening in on the performance.

When little Roger, a boy of 14, saw his father take his hat and start toward the door, he called out, in a tone of regret:

"Oh, papa it's a shame you have to go. The elephants are simply wonderful; the one with the oboe just made a trill in *sol!* Didn't he, Paulette?"

Roger's sister, whose 18 years conferred a musical sense a little less uncertain than that of her brother, corrected him with a smile:

"I think the *sol* was a *re*. But it's true that the elephants are good."

Roger protested:

"A *re*! Never! Women have no ear for music!"

Having delivered himself of this sage maxim, Roger took up his headset again, for the radio in Gribal's apartment, an improvement on the usual models, rendered to perfection the sound of the instruments and voices which are always a little distorted by a loudspeaker.

Madame Gribal, a little less interested than her children in the virtuosos of Calcutta, laid down her listening helmet to say to her husband:

"No overcoat? You'd better take one; the evenings are getting quite chilly now."

Gribal laughed:

"Bah," he said, "it's as warm as a summer's day. Don't worry—this is not a good day for catching colds. Run along back to your concert; I'll be back in a couple of hours, anyway. Have a good time."

"Don't get run over."

Gribal smiled. Every time he went out his wife gave him the same good advice. She knew that her husband was always mulling over some scientific problem in his head, and was quite as likely to stop in the middle of the street to calculate a formula as not. But Gribal had two qualities sufficient to protect even a pedestrian in a city—he had a quick eye, and in spite of his 42 years was as supple and active as a young man of 25; moreover, he was not as absent-minded as he seemed. For he had a sort of double mind; his intelligence went ticking along without in the least interrupting his physical reactions.

And, moreover, what was there to fear? He worked hardly two doors from where he lived, in the Avenue Champs-Elysées, at the Office of Scientific Research, a bureau of the new Ministry of Science. And he had a good position; he was at once the disciple, the friend, and the main reliance of the director of the office, the celebrated Mazelier, the great scientist whose discoveries for the last two years had been upsetting the usual concepts of physics and chemistry.

Gribal had to go up the Champs-Elysées as far as the Rond-Point. He walked gaily along, filled with the

17

joy of life, totting the sweetness of the exquisite autumnal day which seemed meant for a holiday. The engineer, naturally, knew nothing, and could suspect nothing of the drama which was proceeding only a few hundred yards from him, for the dismal announcements of the loudspeaker reached him only as an indistinct murmur. Therefore his surprise was extreme when, as he arrived at the door of the office, he saw the Sun suddenly darkened, and the shadows descend rapidly upon the city.

At first he thought:

"What's this? Night already? My watch must be decidedly slow."

But as rapidly as lightning, another reflection crossed his mind. It was hardly half a minute since he had glanced at the Arc de Triomphe, bathed in sunlight. The Sun was still high above the horizon. No doubt possible; his watch was not slow. But then, what did this sudden darkness mean?

Naturally Gribal was in the habit of searching for a scientific explanation for every phenomenon he observed. This time, to his astonishment, he could not find any.

His stupefaction was such that he expressed it aloud:

"This is too much; I don't believe it," he remarked.

And like any other scientist with a theory upset, he added:

"It's incomprehensible!"

The event that produced such a statement was surprising indeed, for Gribal held it as a fundamental principle that the human mind was capable of understanding everything, and as a consequence accomplishing anything. But, for the moment, there was nothing for it to accomplish. Alone in the Avenue des Champs-Elysées, whose habitual and joyous noises had given place to the silence of the tomb, he was ready to admit that he was dreaming wide awake, and that some kind of an absurd delusion was in possession of his brain.

Suddenly there was a voice at his side, a voice vibrant with inquietude, and which he recognized without difficulty:

"It's you, Gribal? Quick, quick, come here!"

"Ah, you're there, Professor Mazelier?...What the Devil is going on, anyway?"

Gribal felt much reassured. Mazelier was there! The explanation of the phenomenon would not be far behind him. But without replying to Gribal's question, the director of the office repeated, in a voice dominated by a kind of terror:

"Quick! Quick! For Heaven's sake, hurry, Gribal!"

"Wait. I can't see a damned thing. I'm going to light a match."

"No use. Your matches won't light. Here! Take this."

A feeble light, then another, burned suddenly in the shadows. Gribal could make out the face of his superior as he handed him a little torch of singular shape.

"It's a helium lamp," said Mazelier, "the light is resistant to the influence of most kinds of waves. Fortunately, I had a couple with me. But quick, open the laboratory door. You have the key, haven't you? Quick, quick! We haven't a second to lose."

When such a man as Mazelier made a display of uneasiness, there must be some danger both grave and immediate. Gribal ceased asking questions and began acting. He hurried along after his superior, bearing like him, the providential lamp. The two ran through the complex corridors of the laboratory. The sound of a voice was audible, issuing from a loudspeaker placed at one side—the same voice that was carrying terror to all Paris, and doubtless to all the world beside. Gribal paused a moment to hear and grasped a part of the truth. A madman—it could only be a madman—in possession of a frightful power over matter, had conceived the project of annihilating every existing thing.

"In 50 minutes," clamored the voice, "it will be all over with humanity."

50 minutes! The threat had the curious effect of providing Gribal with a clear head and a confidence in his own and his superior's powers. With Mazelier, they would need 50 centuries!

"Ah," he said to Mazelier, "what can I do to help you?"

For he was certain that Mazelier would save the world.

The scientist, leading the way without halting, crossed the laboratory proper where he labored daily surrounded by the juniors of the office. He pushed the door of an inner room where no one was permitted to enter, not even Gribal, who was to a certain extent the depository to whom Mazelier confided his theories, his experiments and his secrets—to draw them forth again, refreshed and altered by the clear intelligence of the engineer.

In this inner room, Mazelier put into practical application his most audacious theories and constructed many pieces of apparatus that had never reached the outer world. But he was a somewhat secretive character; some of his experiments he never mentioned, even to his faithful collaborator, before being certain that the experiment had reached a dead end or would be one more of those successes for which he claimed so little personal credit.

In the latter case, he was in the habit of taking the successful piece of apparatus into the general laboratory, where he revealed its mysteries, and complacently answered the questions of his subordinates. Gribal had never quite dared to question him on what he kept in this mysterious inner room.

He hesitated therefore, at the door of the forbidden chamber, when Mazelier called him:

"Come on, my friend, come along."

Gribal went into the sanctuary, which was sufficiently illuminated by the two helium lamps to make objects visible. To his extreme surprise, he saw no extraordinary pieces of apparatus; there was no arsenal of the sorcerer of modern science he had expected to find. There was only, alone in the whole room, a little table on which was mounted a brilliantly polished sphere of metal—a sphere of copper apparently. Two round legs bore a double ring which encircled the sphere; and in each corner of the table were dials and a maze of little levers; before the sphere itself another dial with a needle on its face indicating the zero point on a scale whose purpose was obscure. That was all. Gribal dared not say, though he thought, that this seemed a very slight apparatus with which to combat the terror of the unknown. But he had not followed his superior to make an argument; he was there to help and to obey.

Feverishly, Mazelier gave the example. He bent busily over the apparatus, his forehead furrowed with frowns, breathing hard. Gribal had never seen him like this before.

Without a word, Mazelier worked one of the levers. As he closed some connection a musical note, low and sustained, came from the sphere, as though it were turning within its supports like an enormous top. But Gribal could perceive that the sphere remained perfectly unmoved. The scientist touched another lever; the sound became sharper and sharper, soared beyond the limit in which the human ear could follow its vibrations. He moved the running members. Suddenly to the sharp, almost intolerable shriek, there succeeded a hammering like the rapid fire of a whole battery of machine-guns! The needle on the dial oscillated, and Mazelier, bending over it, followed its course. It must have satisfied him, for the expression of strain left his face and a sudden flash of pleasure streaked across it.

All the feverishness had disappeared from his motions. He seated himself tranquilly before the little table, and said, in the quiet voice which was his usual manner of speaking:

"Do you know where the enemy of the human species is, Gribal? Not two kilometers west of where we are! Between Passy and the Etoile."

Gribal started and said:

"Can't we do something? Call up the police? Warn the people?"

Mazelier smiled:

"My friend," he said, "begin your research by saying nothing to anybody. To anybody, do you hear? For I do not wish to have to regret confiding in you. And then reflect—this fiend could realize his threat, or at least cause a terrible catastrophe, long before you could find him. I can deal with him more easily from here—perhaps."

An icy hand gripped Gribal's heart. "Perhaps!" His superior had said "Perhaps." Then he was not sure of winning out. The engineer dared to ask:

"I hope you don't believe in the threats of that lunatic?"

Mazelier's reply fell into the little silence:

"Humanity has never been in greater danger. Never! But leave me alone now—I can work better. I still have 30 minutes to do what can be done. It's more than I need... but at a certain moment the defense must move as rapidly as the attack, and you are holding me up. Run along, Gribal; I will try to do it alone."

Gribal could not conceal his emotion:

"My duty is to watch over you," he declared.

"No, no, Gribal. I am running no more risks here than anyone else is running anywhere in Paris. Your duty is to go back home and reassure your family. They must be worried. Run along, Gribal, run along. You can find your way with the lamp. But when you get home, turn on your radio and don't lose a word of what you hear."

What would Gribal not have given to assist, even by his mute presence, in that strange duel in the dark between his superior and the invisible enemy of the human race? But Mazelier's orders were not the kind one discusses.

The engineer, alone and a little frightened, was about to leave when he heard the voice of the unknown—so loud, so close and so clear that Gribal jumped. "Here comes the cold," it said, "the polar cold. In 30 minutes, at most, there will be no more world!"

It was necessary to admit that the unknown was no liar. Both the engineer and the scientist could remark the astonishing and rapid decline in the temperature. But Gribal turned back to find Mazelier's calm unruffled.

"Do you notice," his superior remarked coolly, "that it is becoming easier to breathe?"

Even in the hour of peril his spirit of scientific observation did not desert him. Shivering as he was, Gribal dared to pause for a last question:

"How is it you can hear him so clearly in this inner laboratory? Is there a loudspeaker here?"

"Certainly, my friend. That sphere, which you see before you. It's not metal, it is—but, run along, Gribal! I'll tell you all about it later. Leave me, leave me. Don't hold me up any longer."

Gribal left, his heart constricted, realizing that what he had always thought impossible had occurred; a man, or rather, two men, in possession of the innermost secrets of matter, the one striving to use his knowledge to annihilate it, the other to maintain it in its eternal form. Human intelligence, then, did it dominate all things to such a point?

Gribal found it difficult to admit. Nevertheless, he was a scientist, and the marvels he was witnessing, did they not confirm the most extreme claims science had made? Why not admit, in that case, that matter was vanquished, the secret of atomic and electronic forces discovered at last?

Such ideas filled the mind of the engineer as he hurried homeward at the utmost speed at which his legs would carry him. He was so busy with them that he hardly felt the cold, which was, nevertheless, enough to freeze the hair on a monkey. He hurried along toward the Place de la Concorde, past the Marigny Square and the Avenue Gabriel, all enveloped in night and silence. Not a voice, not a sigh, not the slightest sound in the immense avenue of the Champs-Elysées. 20 minutes had hardly gone by since Gribal, from that same spot, had admired the brilliant light of the Sun and the incomparable spectacle of the Parisian crowd, gay and moving.

What had become of all the strollers, of all the autos that crowded the streets? Paris was deserted.

In the Champs-Elysées the first threats of the unknown, heard at first from the Place de l'Etoile, and in the flicker of an eyelash carried the length of the avenue to the Place de la Concorde, had produced an immediate terror. While Gribal, busy with his thoughts, had been strolling toward the office, walkers, bus-drivers, automobilists, obeying one of those singular mass movements which seize on crowds, had been hastening toward any refuge they could find. What Gribal in his distraction had taken for the ordinary vigorous movement of the avenue's life had been, in reality, a rout, a flight. And the shadows had descended upon the last fliers hastily seeking refuge in the little cross streets.

Meanwhile, as he felt his way along the Avenue Gabriel toward the Rue Boissy d'Anglas, Gribal looked about him to see whether he could not help some person in distress. But he was alone. The feeble light of his lamp was reflected from no human form. Along here everyone had fled, while at the Place de l'Opéra, the curious crowd, victims of their own inquisitiveness, dared no longer make the least effort to disperse.

CHAPTER III
THE GREAT ILLUSION

And it was thus that at a dozen steps from his door, Gribal was seized with a sudden sensation of fear. Would he find his wife and children alive? His wife, Paulette, and Roger? As a scientist, he had faith in the ultimate victory of Mazelier, but as a father, as a man, he feared the worst.

Trembling more with agony than with cold, the engineer hurried into the silent house; the door stood ajar. He mounted the stairs, listening for any noise that would be a sign of life. But one would have said that all the inhabitants of the building were sunk in some supernatural sleep. And Gribal, so anxious to arrive a moment before, now hesitated to unlock the door, nerved himself to the effort and flung it open. At the sound there was a triple exclamation:

"Pierre? Is it you?"

Madame Gribal, as rapidly as she could in the obscurity, ran to her husband, and Roger, suddenly became joyous and confident once more on the arrival of his father, cried out:

"We're in the front room, papa. Wait till I get this chair out of the way, so you won't stumble over it."

Gribal replied from the hallway:

"Stay where you are. I have a light."

Paulette, in her turn, gave a little cry:

"A light! Then we are saved."

His children were worried no longer; their father was there and he was a scientist.

It was just at that moment that the wave of cold became doubly severe though nobody paid any attention as there was a babble of rapid conversation and embraces that ended only when Roger asked:

"Papa, why is it so cold?"

Madame Gribal remarked:

"You see, we've got all the overcoats and furs in the house on. Wait a minute, I'll get you some blankets from the bedroom to wrap yourself in."

"Oh," said Roger, looking at the helium lamp, "what's that?"

"Don't touch it," warned Gribal.

He perceived with satisfaction that it was unnecessary to reassure them. For Roger, the threatened cataclysm was nothing but an exciting adventure. The words transmitted by the loudspeaker had not frightened him at all, for the simple reason that he had not believed them. As for Paulette, who had been for some time her father's most brilliant scientific pupil, she was too curious to be scared. She asked:

"But father, explain to me why we can't light any matches. There is not a light in the streets, and we can't seem to light any of the fires; everything went out in the kitchen. But we are breathing all the same, just like before. So there isn't any lack of oxygen—but why isn't there any combustion?"

The fact had already struck Gribal; for that matter Mazelier had warned him of it; all matches would fail in the midnight atmosphere. But everyone was breathing, full and deep, as though the air of Paris had become suddenly richer in oxygen.

Meanwhile, if Gribal's family had ceased worrying, he himself felt more and more uneasy as the minutes passed. He replied, almost half-heartedly:

"I don't know how to explain it. We will ask Mazelier."

"Did you see Professor Mazelier?"

"Yes."

"Oh, then he must have told you all about it."

Gribal did not think it quite prudent to gratify Paulette's curiosity; and as his children became more and more reassured, his own inquietude, if not his fear, grew greater. The decisive moment was at hand. The prodigious duel would soon be over. But he dared not reveal to his family the existence of that combat, unknown to all but Mazelier, himself, and the mysterious organizer of the catastrophe.

He closed his eyes in spite of himself; then remembered something, and reached for the listening helmet, signing to his wife and children to imitate him.

"Is there something to hear?" asked Roger. "But it's all over, papa."

Gribal insisted:

"Put on your helmets."

"I don't hear anything," murmured Paulette.

"Naturally!" said Roger. "They always cut the most interesting parts. Probably the silly man has gone to get himself warm."

"Do you know?" said Paulette, after a minute, "I think it's less cold than it was."

"Of course," put in Roger, "such a temperature in October is hardly natural. It couldn't last."

At any other time Gribal would have been amused by the superb confidence of his son. How happy the quietude of ignorance was.

Suddenly, the receivers brought the characteristic noise of static that preceded a world-broadcast. Roger remarked:

"Ah, the chap has unfrozen himself! Now he's going to tell us some jokes. You'll see that—"

He did not finish. A cry came to the ears of the listeners, a cry of fury, rage and fright, ending in a sort of desperate rattle. And then, a voice which Gribal had no difficulty in recognizing, pronounced calmly,

"The world is saved. Everything's all right. The danger—"

The sentence was interrupted by a sound which no human being could analyze correctly; resembling, more than anything else, a million electric discharges letting go at once. Then came a complete silence. Gribal imagined that his radio was out of order, some essential part smashed, no doubt, by the combat of radiations between the two adversaries.

Had Mazelier won? Suddenly, all the electric lights of the apartment, which had been switched on, flashed into activity, then died again, as though a sudden burst of current had caused a short-circuit. But the room filled swiftly with light and the helium lamp now looked no more than a candle in the bright glare.

And filled with the joy of victory Gribal cried:

"We are saved! See how the day is coming back!"

He went to open the window, but recoiled, overwhelmed to see in the distance the red light of an enormous conflagration.

The engineer closed the window quicker than he had opened it to shut out the vision. Overwhelmed, he murmured:

"Paris is burning."

Even Roger no longer cared to joke. Paulette, pale, looked into her father's face for some reason for condolence which she did not find there. Madame Gribal was frightened. To the north and east of them the whole city seemed ablaze, with enormous flames roaring up into the skies.

And thus this extraordinary business of night in the middle of day, of winter cold at the beginning of autumn, this boast of the unknown who swore he was going to destroy the Earth, everything that had at first seemed a gigantic conjurer's trick was ending in a genuine drama of fire and ruin.

And what a drama! The world might indeed be saved, but Paris would be destroyed. Radiation of a force and character thus far unknown would not dissolve the planet, but Paris, at the heart of the disturbance, would be itself dissolved by the fire and nothing would remain of the most beautiful city in the world but a pile of ashes.

What had Mazelier and the unknown been doing? The scientist must be in danger, for his announcement of deliverance had been interrupted. He must certainly have tried to break the silence which the other had imposed upon him; he had not succeeded, and the city was afire. Gribal thought but a moment.

"I'm going back to the office," he announced.

"With the city all afire?" said his wife. "I beg you, don't leave us like this."

Worried and stirred by her plea, Gribal hesitated, then became firm. With a resolute reasonableness, he declared:

"Mazelier is in danger. My duty is with him at this moment."

The sacrifice was hard, but there could be no question of the necessity. Madame Gribal, with damp eyes, showed that a Paris wife could show the qualities of a Joan of Arc.

"Go, then," she said. And she added, simply: "Come back as soon as possible, but not before you are sure you can leave."

As she spoke the doorbell rang. Roger ran to open as though the unexpected visitor brought safety itself with him, and Gribal could not repress the feeling that it was no less that, that he brought when Roger returned to announce joyously:

"It's Professor Mazelier!"

Gribal hurried to greet the scientist:

"I was just leaving to come to the office," he cried. "Why do you risk coming all the way here?"

"Risk? I haven't risked anything."

"What? With Paris all afire?"

"Paris afire? Where did you get that idea?"

Gribal opened the window again, pointing toward the Concorde, the Tuileries and the Seine:

"Look, look. It's frightful!"

Mazelier contemplated the flames that had alarmed the engineer and began to laugh:

"There's nothing burning. It's an illusion."

"An illusion?" repeated Gribal, stupefied, but delighted.

"Yes, and the proof is that I am going to take you into the middle of that furnace, I will guarantee that you will be no more exposed to the fire than you are at this moment.

And turning toward Madame Gribal, he added: "I believe I came into your parlor without wishing you good afternoon? Permit me to make my apologies, Madame. And Paulette, how is everything with you? Hello, Roger, I see that you have borne up well under the dark wave and the cold wave we have just been having."

And the boy, at once respectful and familiar, replied like a true child of his age:

"Oh, me, Professor Mazelier, you know how little things like that bother me."

And he added, expressing the feeling that they all felt:

"We knew there was nothing to worry about when we found out you were on the job."

"Ah, you think that—"

"That if something was going to happen, and it didn't happen, it was because you were there to keep it from happening. And that's all there is. It isn't difficult to understand."

Mazelier and Gribal exchanged glances, while Roger went on:

"After all, only a nut would think that the world would come to an end, just like that, while people hadn't had time to finish their lunch—"

"Do you know, Gribal?" said Mazelier, visibly amused by Roger's remarks, "do you know that everybody in Paris will be thinking like that tomorrow, and even more than that? Just as Roger has told us."

"Of course, it couldn't have been anything but some kind of a joke," insisted the boy, "the world didn't come to an end, did it, and there isn't any fire?"

This simple explanation was a long way from being satisfactory to Paulette. The strangeness of the phenomenon had upset her elementary scientific knowledge; if there was really no more danger there still remained a good deal of inexplicable mystery.

Impatient to learn the explanation, she questioned:

"But really, Professor Mazelier, what has been happening? What's going on?"

The scientist was vague: "We'll talk more about it some other day, Paulette. For the moment the scientific problems involved are less interesting than some others. I need Gribal with me, and I must ask your permission to take him away. And if you wish to go out yourself, Madame, don't let anything keep you. There is not the least danger. I repeat it, not the least. You will only have the impression of seeing fireworks all around you, but without any smoke."

"What, everything we see, it isn't—"

"Nothing at all. A coloration of the atmosphere, that's all. An enormous rainbow above us, in such a fashion that we don't see all the colors at once. They will penetrate the air one after another, beginning with the red. It will end with an indigo apparition, so that Paris will be successively enveloped in purple, topaz, emerald, sapphire and amethyst. And then the Sun will come back and it will be all over."

"All over," said Gribal, with a little retrospective shudder.

"Yes, all over—for this time," added Mazelier in a voice which only his companion heard.

Neither Roger, Paulette, nor Madame Gribal heard these last words. Only Gribal grasped their significance, and they brought him back with a start to reality, reminding him that Professor Mazelier's tranquil air was assumed to impress the others. But why did he thus seem to encourage such incredulity and joking references as Roger's? And why, Gribal asked himself, this grave reserve behind, those mysterious words "for this time?"

In any case, there was one gain. The catastrophe announced by the radio had thinned out into a series of queer atmospheric effects. The affair had not ended badly—thanks to Mazelier, the silent victor in the unknown

33

and terrible struggle. What a singular situation! An hour ago, seeing Mazelier go by, a little round-shouldered man with graying hair and a little beard cut to a point in the old-fashioned manner, no one in the world would have selected him as the savior of humanity. He would have been passed by with a glance and a remark—"That old chap? Looks like one of those goofy professors, with those thick glasses."

But behind those glasses, few would have observed that the eyes were young and modest, too modest to seek public applause for anything the brain behind them conceived.

But Gribal knew. He wished to cry out, to tell the world:

"Ah," he said, "what would have happened to all of us if—"

Mazelier interrupted him brusquely.

"Come along. We'll be late. You must hurry if you want to get back in time for dinner; we have a lot to do. And then Madame Gribal would not pardon me, and what a fix you would have me in."

The scientist accompanied these words with a wink so unmistakable that Gribal understood at once that he was to say nothing. He shrugged his shoulder: "All right, I'm ready any time."

"Let's go, then. We have a rather delicate calculation to make at the office."

A calculation! Nothing would have pleased Gribal better under the circumstances. He knew without a word being said that the calculation had something to do with the mysterious promoter of the end of the world.

At the corner of the Rue Boissy d'Anglas and the Avenue Gabriel, with the immense panorama of the empty Place de la Concorde and the Seine spread before them, Mazelier suddenly gripped his assistant by the arm:

"Look," he said, "what do you see there?"

CHAPTER IV
THE FIRST CLUE

Gribal made no effort to restrain his cry of astonishment. To the flamboyant red along the skyline, which had so frightened him before, there had succeeded an orange fog, light and transparent, here and there thinning off into clear yellow as though the rays of the Sun were trying to pierce it.

"It is exactly as you predicted," declared the engineer. "But I confess that I don't understand why."

Mazelier smiled a little quiet smile.

"And I am willing to bet that you imagine I understand everything that is beyond your depth? Alas! my ignorance is almost as complete as your own. For what's the use predicting something when the reason why it is taking place is unknown to you?"

And with the same expression of a half-smile which accentuated the expression of a good-natured old professor he habitually wore, he added: "Listen, Gribal, try to put yourself inside the head of the individual about whom we won't know anything till we've read tomorrow's newspapers."

"Tomorrow's papers. You're joking."

"Not a joke. We're reasoning in a vacuum—at least until we have news from all over the world. What has been happening in Paris is only a detail. We need the complete picture."

"But," objected Gribal, "the newspapers know as little as we do. In fact, they know less; nobody has any idea of what you've been doing. Instead of getting exact information by tomorrow we will be drowned in thousands of bughouse lies."

"Bah! We will try to read between the lines. But do you notice, my dear Gribal, that we are alone, absolutely alone, on the Champs-Elysées. Our countrymen have not dared to stick their noses out yet. They're going to laugh at each other soon. Here we are, at last. But who is that pulling up at the office?"

A powerful car, emerging from the cape of fog which was already taking on a greenish hue, had halted, not indeed, before the main entrance to the office, but a few yards further along at the corner of the Rue de la Boëtie. A tall man, with a soft felt hat pulled down over his nose and a scarf that concealed his chin, leaped swiftly from the vehicle, took several steps toward the office, and then, his eye falling on Mazelier and Gribal, turned, and leaped back into the auto.

"Wrong address," said Gribal, with a laugh, "you'll find the bar a little further down the street, old man."

The explanation apparently did not satisfy Mazelier. The engineer heard him grumbling:

"And why should that car drive up and then go off again as soon as we get here?"

"Pure coincidence. Anyhow, we have seen the first auto that has been moving in Paris since the end of the world. That's one rarity at least."

This mild pleasantry had no effect on Mazelier. Before entering he turned again to look after the car, which was moving rapidly away in the direction of the Rond-Point.

"And not a cop in sight to pinch him for speeding," said Gribal. "Whether this fog is green or not it is certainly a fog; that chauffeur ought to switch his lights on."

"The chauffeur?" asked Mazelier. "By the way, did you get a good look at that chauffeur?"

"No, why should I look at him?"

"I'll bet anything he is a Chinese. A pure Manchu."

"The Devil!" exclaimed Gribal. "We're in the fashionable world. A Chinese chauffeur, that's something clever."

"Anyway," replied Mazelier energetically, "his employer was not afraid of the fire, like you."

Gribal was impressed by the accent of the scientist. What did he have up his sleeve? He risked a sharp answer to draw his superior's ideas:

"If he wasn't afraid of the fire, what's more natural than that he should take a little ride around the town? We're doing the same thing, only on foot."

Mazelier shook his head:

"Listen, Gribal. Would we have gone out if we were not sure that we would find nothing wrong in the streets of Paris? But who informed that chap there that everything was all right? How did he know what we are the only ones to know?"

The engineer was silent, struck by the force of the observation. Mazelier went on, jerking along at a nervous stride in a manner that showed his preoccupation as he spoke:

"Therefore the man in the big car must be an accomplice of the bandit whom we are trying to discover. And what if it were he, himself? He, whom we have seen…"

The engineer had followed his superior into the inner laboratory as they talked, eager to assist at the calculation the latter had promised him; that remarkable calculation, which had so much and so extraordinary an importance. For he did not doubt that Mazelier would reveal to him the double secret of the attempt to destroy the world and the means by which he had overcome the destroyer.

"My friend," said the scientist, "we are about to work on a document of the first importance. Come over here; turn on that commutator. Good... Can you see clearly?"

"That map? But it is a map of Paris."

"Certainly. It's a map of Paris. Did you expect something else?"

"I admit it."

"And I understand why. Only, my dear Gribal, what worries me at this particular moment is not the nature of the phenomena we have been seeing. There are no theories to be deduced from them, nor any warnings for the future that we can draw from them. We can do all that sort of thing later—if we have time. Today, we must work at top speed."

"That is to say—"

"That is to say that we must first discover who it was who tried to destroy the Earth, and at any cost, at any cost whatever—do you understand?—keep him from trying it again. For if we leave him alone he is sure to have another whirl at it, Gribal."

And lowering his voice instinctively, Mazelier added: "And he might be stronger than us the second time."

Gribal protested by shaking his head.

"No! A thousand times no, Professor! Don't exaggerate the powers of that man. Don't underestimate your own abilities—you have just beaten him at every point."

"No doubt. I have beaten him, as you say. But how badly? We can only tell later. And while we are waiting—to work, my dear Gribal."

"But," protested the engineer, "the unknown must necessarily work alone. It is impossible to imagine that anyone would help him in such an enterprise. No matter how mad he is, he certainly would not have confided in anyone. While we—"

"While we? Well, well, Gribal; go on, finish your sentence."

"We have all the police forces of the world, all the civilized governments, everyone to whom we choose to appeal. With so much help we could surmount any difficulty."

"You fool, don't you understand? Don't you know what your contemporaries are like? Tell the world about the existence of the unknown, make it known that instead of a joke he really meant business, and all the imaginations in the world will go to work. An army of madmen, of criminals, of unknowns, will spring up, will be arrested on every hand. We should never find the real criminal. And depend upon it, our unknown has taken good precautions to prevent just such a public search."

"But, Professor, what then?"

"Then we must get busy ourselves, my dear Gribal, with our own resources; we must search him out ourselves. A long and difficult task no doubt. Of course, the police could set up the same inquiries we could—less secretly, naturally. But they have two faults; this is a scientific problem and they know nothing of science, and they lack the necessary persistence. By tomorrow the police themselves will be issuing statements that there has been nothing serious going on. If I contradicted them, they would laugh—and all the other police forces in the world would laugh in chorus with them."

And rapping out his words, Mazelier went on with his tirade:

"It's up to us to undertake the job. And it is a dangerous job, don't kid yourself on that point. We will risk everything we have, our lives and the lives of everyone we touch. We can ask help from no one, we must beware of everyone in the world. If we go down, no one will even know, and if we succeed, I fear there will be no applause for us. Under such conditions, Gribal," are you prepared to go on with me? There is still time to say no."

For his only reply Gribal bent over the map of Paris that Mazelier had showed him.

"I am ready," he said. "What shall I do?"

"Simply this. Get yourself a compass, a ruler and a pencil. Good. Of course you know that just now my first care was to find out from precisely what point the cold and dark radiation was coming; or rather, the interruption in the radiation of light and heat. Well, we will follow out on this map the course I have traced by means of my implements."

Mazelier drew from his pocket a sheaf of notes.

"Here Find the place where we are now; Rue de la Boëtie, at the corner of the Avenue. Now, trace along the line of the Rue Pierre Charron a line 900 meters long, on the scale of the map."

"Done."

"Where are we?"

"Place d'Iéna."

"Place d'Iéna. Remarkable! I imagined a little while ago that I had made a mistake in saying at first that the source of the trouble was between Passy and the Etoile. But now I imagine that we will not have to look elsewhere. Now Gribal, at the end of your line draw a perpendicular 300 meters long on the same scale. We are…?"

"At the corner of Rue de Lubeck."

41

"Good. Rue de Lubeck. Ah, there's something wrong about here; I almost lost the trail. Something happened of which I'm not quite certain. But I tuned in on another circuit. At the extremity of the perpendicular of 300 meters, make another of about 1000 meters long. Wait, that's it! Hold it there, Gribal. Where's the spot?"

"Rue Cortambert, near the Place de la Muette."

The two men looked at each other, a little pale.

Mazelier was the first to speak. "We must go there, Gribal."

And almost thoughtfully, he added, "The Rue Cortambert! One of the quietest and most aristocratic streets in the quiet and aristocratic quarter of Passy."

"Yes," said Gribal, following his thought, "it seems impossible that the person we are looking for has not been noticed in a district of that kind. If only by the size and importance of his laboratory."

"True. True. At least, if... *Parbleu!* At least if he has not succeeded, like me, in simplifying his machine to an extraordinary degree. But why should he not have discovered the same things I have?"

Gribal had a thousand questions on the tip of his tongue, but he kept silent, knowing that his superior was not yet ready to answer them. For that matter, there would hardly have been time. As Mazelier rose, preparing to go, there was a knock at the door of the laboratory.

Mazelier frowned. Who was daring to interrupt in spite of the strict orders he had given that he should not be disturbed? Gribal went to the door and found Père Bibent, the old concierge of the office.

"What is it, Père Bibent? You know very well that Professor Mazelier will not see anyone when he is busy in his laboratory."

"I beg your pardon, Monsieur Gribal. But it is a young electrician who says he'll tear the place apart if he doesn't see Professor Mazelier. He insists he has something of the utmost urgency and importance to tell you. Here he comes, now. He looks honest, so I ventured—"

Gribal, in spite of his annoyance, could not repress a smile. Poor old Bibent! He imagined himself a psychologist.

But the indiscreet visitor pushed Bibent aside, and with the desperate hurry of the very timid, addressed Gribal, speaking rapidly:

"Monsieur, I have a revelation to make concerning the events which have just been happening. Pardon me for interrupting you, but I must tell you about it. It's important."

Gribal regarded the unknown. The young workman really did look honest, and his air, at once modest and decided, spoke in his favor.

Bibent was eclipsed and vanished across the laboratory in the direction of the door whose watch-dog he was.

Gribal set himself to put a few preliminary questions:

"What is your name?"

"Monsieur, my name is Roland Duplay. I'm an electrician, and I have just finished my course at the Breguet school."

"And why did you come here instead of going to the police?"

"Monsieur, because what happened this afternoon is so extraordinary that only a scientist like Professor Mazelier can find the explanation for it."

"And you have something to tell him?"

"Yes, Monsieur. I know who it was who declared he would destroy the world."

"Well, who was it?"

"It was the Marquis de Saint-Imier, who lives in the Rue Cortambert."

"Rue Cortambert!"

Instead of barring the door before the young workman Gribal seized him by the shoulders and literally pushed him into the laboratory.

"Quick, speak, my boy. Tell us everything you know. Did you hear, Mazelier? Rue Cortambert!"

Mazelier gazed calmly at the newcomer without the slightest surprise. He asked coolly: "How do you know?"

Duplay replied: "I was at the Place de l'Opéra when the voice came through the loudspeaker. I got as close as I could to it to hear better. And I swear to you that I recognized the voice. It was not two weeks ago that I was doing some work at the Marquis' house. I was astonished at the things he had me install there. And his voice, Monsieur! It's impossible to forget it when one has heard it a single time. That man frightened me, Monsieur. It could only be him."

"But you should go tell that to the police, my boy."

"They wouldn't believe me, Monsieur. The Marquis is rich, he has a lot of pull, everybody knows him. They wouldn't even listen to me at the police. They'd tell me I was crazy. While you, you are a scientist, you can tell whether I'm right or not."

"And why should I know any better than the police?"

"Because you're a scientist. I have read your books, Monsieur,—oh, if I could only understand them better. I have followed everything you have done."

Gribal and Mazelier exchanged a glance.

"Thank you, my boy," said the scientist. "And what can I do for you?"

"I don't dare ask for any reward," babbled Duplay. "I'm so ignorant."

Mazelier divined the thoughts that were agitating the young electrician.

"Well, Monsieur Duplay," he said, accenting the word *Monsieur*, "I advise you to stick to your profession, but if you have any leisure time you may employ it at this office if you wish. Gribal will show you the research we are carrying on, if you think you would like to see them."

Overwhelmed with emotion and gratitude, the workman stood before them, incapable of pronouncing a single word. But his attitude and his glance showed that the two scientists had gained the undying devotion of the young man.

"Now," said the scientist, "one last question. Here's a map of Paris. Would you mind showing us the exact point where the Marquis' house, where you made the installation, stands?"

Duplay bent over the map. Then with a visible astonishment:

"It's exactly at the point that is marked with a blue cross."

And he looked up with wondering eyes.

"Did you know, then?"

"Faith!" said Mazelier, "we know what hole he was in, but we didn't know the name of the rat. Good, Monsieur Duplay, you may come back here whenever you like. I have the conviction that you will be a scientist someday."

The electrician bade them farewell, his face alight.

"Do you think he's all right?" asked Gribal.

"Entirely! And now, let's go have a look at the Rue Cortambert. It will be a nice little walk, and I am curious."

Gribal glanced out into the Avenue.

"The Sun has come back," he announced. "Look, look! What a crowd. What animation!"

"Yes, of course. Everyone knows it was only some kind of a joke or nightmare now. They're all telling each other how brave they were."

CHAPTER V
NEW DEVELOPMENT

He was not far wrong; it was the end of the night-mare. One would have said that every inhabitant of the great city had come out to salute the return of the light of day in a public and universal joy like that of some grand holiday. For a few moments the people of Paris seemed strangely purified; their delight, their happiness bade farewell to all hatred, envy and despair as a breeze drives away a pestilential mist.

From the Etoile to the Concorde a human tide flowed without ebb. Mazelier and Gribal even had some difficulty in making their way through the crowded streets.

"Ah," said the engineer, "this makes the Sun-worship of the barbarous ages comprehensible."

"Yes," said Mazelier, "but just at the present moment I would be more appreciative of the benefits of civilization in the form of a bus."

"But look how everybody is moving around," cried Gribal. "Decidedly the Parisians are easy to reassure. Here, let's get up to the Boulevard Haussmann and take the electric."

The electric monorail car, quick, light and silent, which ran from the Carrefour Drouot to the Muette, was right on their route. 15 minutes later the two amateur detectives descended at the Avenue Henri-Martin, near the Rue Cortambert.

Mazelier explained:

"There are enough people in the streets so that we won't be noticed. We'll go along slowly as though we were out for a stroll. Unless I'm much mistaken, we will know very quickly when we come to an interesting place."

"And how will we know?"

"Oh, a little trick of my own, Gribal. Look, this will give us the signal."

Mazelier drew from his pocket a little round object.

"What's that? A watch? And how will that signal us?" asked the engineer, surprised.

"It's rather like a watch, true. But it isn't one all the same. There's a little buzzer inside—oh, a very little one—that will sound when we get close to the emission source of any unusual wave radiations. If, as I expect, our adversary is still at work, it will reveal his presence, and we will know both where he lives and where he carries on his labors. Look, I'm going to wind it up; that will set it to catch any radiation."

Mazelier had put on a different pair of spectacles and held in his hand a sporting journal in which he seemed to be deeply interested as he strolled along. For the passers-by he was the perfect model of a little shopkeeper intensely interested in the outcome of the bicycle races, but whose personal devotion to athletics does not extend beyond a two-block walk after dinner.

As for Gribal, he lighted a cigar and assumed the air of a boulevardier whose ambition is limited to eating two well-chosen meals a day and making the circuit of the most famous cafés of Paris for a drink in each afterward. Both of them paid no attention to each other. These precautions were hardly exaggerated, considering the fact that they knew nothing either of the ability of their adversary or his means of defense. His means of defense?—rather, his means of attack.

Thus they arrived at what Gribal called the "hot spot." Mazelier slackened his pace, and then halted, holding his watch to his ear like a man who doubts whether it is in running order. And his face showed a lively surprise, followed by some irritation.

He went on to the end of the street, followed at a little distance by Gribal, who understood that the apparatus invented by his superior was not giving the hoped-for result. Had Mazelier made a mistake in the house? No, for he had turned back and resumed his patrol before the same building.

All at once the bugle of a large auto sounded a blare of notes, and people crossing the street leaped out of the way of a huge car which arrived at high speed, pulled up suddenly and swung through a double gate that opened to receive it. The auto was swallowed up in the inner court of the mansion; a building decorated in the most sumptuous style, but too modern in character to catch the eye of an artist.

On the sidewalk, near Mazelier and Gribal, two passers-by halted to watch the entrance of the big car.

"Who's that?" asked one of them.

"Don't you know?" asked the other in the superior tone a butler in a grand household would employ in informing a new porter of his duties. "That's the Marquis de Saint-Imier. There's a chap who doesn't worry about a thing—even the end of the world don't keep him from running around the town."

Gribal felt someone nudge his elbow. Mazelier motioned him to follow at a little distance.

"Did you see?"

"*Parbleu!*" said the engineer, "the chauffeur was a Chinese."

"Did you recognize the car?"

"I recognized the chauffeur even more vividly."

"Wait a minute."

Suddenly Gribal jumped. The sound of a little buzzer came sharply to his ear, causing him more fright than the voice of terror on the loudspeaker.

"All right, daughter?"

"I should say so, father. And you, mother? We ought to amuse ourselves a little from time to time; we have had so much to worry about. Are you coming with us?"

Madame Gribal was slightly scandalized:

"Me? To go to a reception at the ministry? You're crazy, child. I'd be bored to death. And who would get your lunch for you?"

"Ah, that wouldn't matter. For once in our lives we could do with some chocolate and cakes."

"Yes, yes. It's easy to say that beforehand, but when the moment came I think you'd want something a little more substantial. No, no, run along with your father to the reception. I'll stay home and take care of Roger."

"Thanks very much, but I don't need it," said the young man of whom she spoke.

But Gribal came to the rescue of the maternal authority:

"You stay home, young man. You'll see too much of receptions and ministries when you grow up. But you can go to the movies tomorrow, and let Paulette get lunch for you."

Paulette was genuinely enchanted with the invitation to the reception, which had arrived no later than that morning. Even a girl whose heart is set on becoming a scientist sometimes enjoys putting on her best dress and going to parties. She found the Minister of Science a delightful person and was quite prepared to vote him into office for life. She was even so happy over the prospect that she forgot the mysteries of the day before and the scientific questions they aroused and which she was so anxious to resolve with her father. Paulette was not ignorant of the fact that the Minister of Science was at once a politician of some prominence and well known in the fashionable world. His invitations were as much in demand among the smart set as among the universities.

But Paulette could not but wonder why the Minister of Science should organize one of his most elaborate receptions on the very day after the extraordinary event which had alarmed all Europe for the space of several hours.

Gribal thought he understood, but said nothing. He had talked the matter over with Mazelier, also one of those on the invitation list. But the scientist had told him:

"I don't think I'll go. I will hear so many stupid remarks that I would end up by laughing in their faces, and being in an official position I haven't the right to laugh. You go, Gribal. Look around you, listen to everything they say. If you find out anything interesting, you can give me the news at the office tomorrow."

"Don't you think it a little—premature, this idea of the Minister's, of having a kind of *fête* so soon after the attack of the unknown?"

"My dear Gribal, I think the Minister is perfectly right. I'm going to tell you the truth—in official quarters they are absolutely terrified. They don't understand in the least what has happened. They only want to reassure the public, and what better means than a big society reception as though it were all nothing to worry about? It will be a fete in honor of Science—do you get the idea? In the honor of Science, which defends, protects, and sometimes ultimately explains the inexplicable. The Minister is pretending a tranquility which he is really very far from feeling."

"Did you see him?"

Mazelier smiled slightly.

"Now do you really doubt it? The Minister summoned a whole army of meteorologists in the greatest urgency yesterday evening. There was a great deal of discussion about currents in the upper atmosphere, the Heaviside Layer, the effect of charges of electricity on abnormal atmospheric depressions. And as nobody understood what anybody else was saying, they wound up by cooking up a story to issue to the public. When you get to the heart of it, it is quite meaningless. Oh, a good story, you understand…Something about a wireless amateur who got the atmospheric electrical currents all tangled up, and who has now been arrested."

"But," cried Gribal, "such a yarn can't be believed for a moment. And the cold? And the sudden darkness? And the impossibility to make any light? And—"

"Yes, yes," said Mazelier, "all of that. But you forget that the crowd forgets quickly and thinks not at all."

"Good. Suppose we admit that. But even the crowd reads the newspapers. And the newspapers this morning had the news that the cold wave spread over all the eastern district of France and most of the rest of Europe, beginning with the meridian of Paris. We know that the wave of darkness did the same and only ended at the line that passes through Riga and the tip of Greece. We know that west of Paris nobody noticed any effect except that all the wireless sets went out of order. But how in the world can anybody take the combination of all these phenomena for a mere joke? Who would believe it?"

"Who? Everybody. The public has become used to the marvelous. When there is some new miracle every day, you get bored with the next one very quickly, and end up by not paying attention to any of them"

"Don't you wish to see the Minister and tell him what you know?"

"Once more, no! And after all, what do I know? Reflect, Gribal. What do we really know? Just what the papers have printed, no more. Three quarters of Paris felt the effects of the cold and dark waves. Auteuil and the Bois de Boulogne were only relatively dark. Further west the Sun went right on shining. And then?"

"Then," said Gribal, "I deduce that someone in the Rue Cortambert succeeded in—"

"Oh, yes. The Marquis de Saint-Imier. The moment has certainly not come to reveal what we have discovered or even to be sure of the guilt of a man we have never seen. Go to the reception, Gribal, amuse yourself. I doubt whether you will find the key to the mystery at the Ministry of Science however."

"And you, Professor, what will you be doing?"

"Me? I'll work. At least up to midnight. See you tomorrow, but be careful who you talk to about it."

The engineer, although obedient to Mazelier's advice, could not resist the impression that he was overcautious. Why should he, Gribal, in an assembly which would include the most eminent and respected scientists of the country, be careful about whom he talked to? There would be women there, naturally, but none of the women one would find at a ministerial reception would be at all likely to even understand a scientific theory. He determined to establish himself in some quiet corner and watch what went on, obeying Mazelier's command to the extent of not talking about anything with anybody.

Paulette, naturally, was in an entirely different state of mind. Her pleasure had no alloy. Arriving at the ministry, she was at first a little frightened by all the splendors, to which she was a such a stranger, but a Parisian of Paris itself, her embarrassment was only momentary.

Besides, chance brought her under the eye of one of her school professors in the very first moment, and before she had time to think about it had been presented to ten different people and drawn into the midst of a particularly interesting conversation.

"I assure you," Madame Reynier-Vitral was saying, "that my husband doesn't see anything at all extraordinary in what happened yesterday."

"Really!" exclaimed a woman who had a doctor's degree and lost no opportunity of letting people know it. "What sort of thing must happen to astonish a chemist?"

"But the affair yesterday was nothing but a kind of chemical experiment that could be reproduced any time one wished."

There was a unanimous chorus of protest. A woman lawyer's voice rose above the rest:

"Oh, do tell your husband not to repeat the experiment right away, please! What jolly jokes these chemists make—to turn our temperature into 40 degrees below zero on a moment's notice."

"Without mentioning that it was so dark you could cut it with a knife," added Madame Brasseur. "To be cold, that's all right, we can understand it, but not to be able to see people's teeth chatter—it's absolutely ill-bred."

Senator Moutonneau intervened:

"But, dear lady," he said to the lawyer, "who told you that it was 40 below? I'm certain that it was a lot nearer 80."

"Impossible!" said the learned dame, impolitely.

"But, asking your pardon a thousand times, it is not only possible, it happened."

"Oh, Monsieur, I will pardon you ten-thousand times, but not for your 80 degrees below zero. But look—we wouldn't be here talking if it had been that cold, we would all be dead."

"It's a singular fact," remarked Monsieur Perignon, "that there has been no epidemic as the result of the cold wave—not even a single case of bronchitis."

"Which proves that the human body can support extremely reduced temperatures."

"Impossible!" declared the doctor again. "I know from my personal experience how easy it is to catch a cold."

Paulette ventured timidly to toss a question onto this sea of conversation:

"But what was the cause of the dark and the cold?"

"Well," said Madame Reynier-Vitral, "according to my husband it was this way—it was a question simply of the absorption of light by the agitated electrons of matter. The American physicist Millikan,[3] in 1927, predicted the possibility of such phenomena."

But nothing in this ordinary banal drawing-room conversation predicted what was to follow a few minutes later.

---

[3] Robert A. Millikan (1868-1953), American experimental physicist and Nobel laureate for his measurement of the charge on the electron and for his work on the photoelectric effect. (Ed.)

Nevertheless, Paulette had a vague presentiment of something about to happen, for which she could not account.

She insisted: "Good. That answers for the dark. But the cold?"

"Couldn't that be explained by an almost total absorption of the light in the upper atmosphere, thus producing a drop in the temperature?"

But Paulette, now less bashful, plunged on with the question she had already put to her father: "But, Madame, how do you explain how we managed to breathe while all combustion had become impossible?"

Everybody looked toward the wife of the chemist. As a matter of fact all had noticed it; nobody had been able to relight the lights that had gone out. Therefore, there was no oxygen for combustion. Then how was it that every being plunged into that sinister and sudden night had had the impression of breathing more deeply and freely instead of succumbing at once to a lack of oxygen?

Madame Reynier-Vitral, fortified with the science of her husband, did not hesitate a second: "My husband," she said with becoming modesty, "thinks that radioactive gases were somehow set free in the atmosphere yesterday. Everywhere in the laboratories they were following the experiments of Messieurs Bayeux and Vaugeois. Therefore the composition of the air was modified, but without being changed in a fashion dangerous to living beings. The proof is that we could live in the modified atmosphere."

CHAPTER VI
THE SECRET EXPOSED

This explanation, which really explained nothing at all, enthused Paulette. She believed she saw the first rays of the light of truth. And why should it not be possible, in the secrecy of the laboratory, to create and then to spread abroad, unknown gases, rays up to now unfamiliar since their number and power of expansion was theoretically infinite?

Nevertheless, Monsieur Perignon was not at all satisfied. He spoke slowly:

"I would like to know what Monsieur Gribal thinks about all this."

And, addressing himself to Paulette, he added, "Your father must have made some observations on the affair?"

The young girl was about to reply when she was interrupted by an occurrence. Monsieur Perignon's question had been heard by a personage whose elegance, at once athletic and aristocratic, was remarkable even in that assemblage. His face was expressive and his eyes almost incredibly active. There was a sort of concentrated irony in his smile as he approached Senator Moutonneau, and asked:

"Gribal? Who is that Gribal? I don't remember having heard that name before."

The senator replied, loudly enough to be heard by the whole group: "That name, my dear Marquis, belongs to a man of the first rank. Gribal is the principal collaborator of the famous Professor Mazelier."

"Mazelier! Faith, I didn't know that he was so famous. In any case, that young lady is certainly a beauty—hardly what one would expect of the daughter of a scientist."

And the man who had been addressed as a Marquis, went on, with a little laugh: "Tell me, Senator, if someone succeeded in disassociating matter, wouldn't it be a shame to dissolve such a beautiful assembly of atoms as Mademoiselle Gribal?"

Had this rather impertinent speech been made deliberately in a tone of voice a little loud? In any case, the reflection was distinctly audible to Paulette's ears. The young girl blushed, then turned her back to hide her chagrin at the remark, by which she was not at all flattered.

But the Marquis, as though he had not noticed her annoyance, advanced toward the group with the ease of a man of the world whom nothing upsets. He saluted Madame Muserolle and extended his hand to Professor Perignon. Then, excusing himself for having interrupted the conversation, he bowed before Paulette with a courtesy that was more than a trifle exaggerated.

"I believe I overheard them addressing some very interesting questions to you?" he said in a tone of inquiry.

"Yes," said the senator, "they were asking her what Monsieur Gribal had thought of the events of yesterday."

All eyes turned toward Paulette, and she felt as though she had never in her life so much desired to give a sharp answer to anyone: *How can you find the observations of a man you never heard of interesting?*

But instead of saying the words that leaped to her lips, she lifted her eyes to those before her and saw them so attentive, so respectful, so little like what the remark had led her to expect that she felt ashamed for her thoughts. After all, he was also one of the Minister's guests. She replied, a little confused: "I don't think my father made any special observations. In fact, I am sure he didn't."

And she went on, rather naively: "If he did make any, he hasn't communicated them to me." Was it possible that what she had just said seemed to afford a certain pleasure to the Marquis? But Monsieur Moutonneau lifted his head:

"It is impossible that a man of Gribal's intelligence should not have made some extremely interesting notes in a case like this."

"Really?" inquired the Marquis in a tone that contained a good deal of sarcasm.

But Paulette did not perceive the undertone.

"Certainly!" declared the senator positively. "Gribal would not know whether it was 40 degrees below zero or 80, but he has, I am willing to wager, some extremely interesting opinions on the dissociation of the atom and the destruction of matter."

"Brrr!" said the lady doctor. "Let's talk about something else."

"Let's not," said the Marquis. "Tell me some more about it, I beg you. I am as ignorant as a herring, and would like to obtain a little information while I'm in such scientific company. You think it's possible to destroy matter completely?"

"Oh," cried Paulette, carried along into the discussion in spite of herself, and excited by having her father's name dragged into the conversation, "Oh, it's just impossible."

The Marquis cast her a furious glance, but it was in a suave voice and with the most charming smile that he replied:

"Ah, really, mademoiselle! I am glad to hear that Monsieur Gribal thinks so."

"My father has always told me that to dissociate matter is not to annihilate it."

Monsieur Perignon approved:

"*Parbleu!*" he said, "evidently an atom dissociated into its electrons is not destroyed any more than a piece of sugar that has been dissolved in coffee. Only a madman could dream of the destruction of the world."

Paulette, delighted at this approval, went on:

"Certainly. Matter once dissociated, resolved into its simplest form, which is energy, would simply reform in another shape, and that's all."

The Marquis seemed pensive:

"But," he objected, "if I understand what you are saying, Mademoiselle, if one dissociated matter, it would simply result in the creation of a new world. Faith, the one we are living in is so poorly made, that it's almost worth the trouble of doing it to get a new one."

And he added, laughing:

"Don't you think so?"

There was no echo of his gaiety. Paulette had a sensation that his laugh had something grating and unpleasant in it. And that voice, with its curious vibrating inflections, where had she heard it before? She felt a disagreeable impression, as one does in the presence of people one detests instinctively.

She watched the Marquis slyly from the corner of her eye—an art which all girls possess from the cradle upwards. The result rather astonished her. He radiated an atmosphere of superior intelligence; his eyes yielded to no one's. But there was something vaguely antipathetic about him.

All at once Paulette found the key of it; the emotion he aroused in anyone who looked at him was fear.

But the doctor was speaking:

"Well, you can make your new worlds in the laboratory if you wish. I admit that I did not find the remaking of this one a pleasant affair. The darkness that came on the city last night found me at the door of a client with no way of getting in."

"And you, my dear senator?" asked Madame Reynier-Vitral.

"The Senate was in session at the Luxembourg, Madame. We simply waited calmly, for it is the duty of the French Senate to give an example of calmness to the world."

The Marquis suggested: "You didn't even try to telephone home?"

Monsieur Moutonneau admitted; "We did think of it. But the telephones weren't working."

"And at the Chamber of Deputies?"

"*Peuh!* They say that some of the deputies were really terrified."

"Oh, the deputies," said the doctor, "they're young. The senators for my choice." And she smiled archly.

Then, she turned toward the Marquis: "And you?" she said, "what did you do about those uncomfortable phenomena and the threats on the radio?"

Paulette glanced at the man thus addressed:

"Me, Madame?" said the Marquis, "I am sorry to admit it, but I saw nothing. I was in the Bois de Boulogne. At a certain moment it seemed to me that it became a trifle chilly, and I came back to Paris too late—like the police. The show was over."

"You didn't even see the discoloration of the atmosphere? It was really superb."

The Marquis replied dryly:

"No, Madame. I missed the whole thing."

He put into that simple phrase a certain intonation of profound distaste, almost of anger. But he recovered with wonderful quickness, and added in a tone too lively not to be sincere:

"It's queer. I, who saw nothing at all, I am more astonished than you who were in the middle of Paris. I see the whole thing less clearly than you, Madame Brasseur, in front of your client's door in the dark. The events of yesterday seem so incomprehensible. And what is queerer still is the way everyone talks about it. Look—I'm not dreaming am I? I'm really in a circle of the greatest scientists of France? Well, when they told me about yesterday, I thought they were having a joke at my expense. I said it was impossible. Now you others, ladies and gentlemen, you are scientists, you say that it was possible, and you add, if I understand this, that it was simply a sort of laboratory joke. Is that correct?"

"Faith," said Perignon, "hardly. I think as you do—it was impossible."

The Marquis smiled. But it seemed to Paulette that his color changed. The senator remarked in a serious tone: "It's a good thing you came to this reception. Now, if the world does come to an end, you will understand why."

"You are right, my dear senator. As you say, I'll understand why next time. I'm glad I was a boyhood friend of the Minister of Science, for he certainly did not invite me here because of my knowledge."

And in a new burst of his mad humor, the Marquis went on:

"Then the only thing certain about it is that yesterday some millions of human beings were convinced that

62

they were about to perish. Unfortunately, most of them were unable to see the senators giving an example of calmness to the world. Well, since we have arrived at the moment for confidences, perhaps Mademoiselle Gribal will tell us her impressions?"

It was said in a perfectly natural manner. Paulette carelessly—for why should she be on her guard—replied with her ordinary frankness:

"*Mon Dieu!* I was more interested than disturbed, I assure you."

"Brave child!"

"My brother jokes all the time. And he was particularly amusing when he put on mother's old coat to protect himself against the cold. And we were all very much reassured when father arrived with his little lighted lamp.

The Marquis gave a start of surprise so marked that the others gazed at him.

"Ah!" he said, "your father—"

"Father had a helium lamp that Professor Mazelier gave him. And then, it was Professor Mazelier who explained to us that the red light was not caused by a big fire as we thought."

"Ah!" babbled the Marquis, "that Professor Maz—"

He did not finish his sentence. His smile gave place to a kind of convulsive and horrible grin, and he became so pale that the doctor said:

"Do you feel ill?"

But the Marquis was not one of those to be so easily overthrown. He bowed to Madame Brasseur:

"It is a trifle warm here," he remarked. "Thank you, Madame, but I shall not need your help this time."

At this moment an eddy of the crowd formed around the entry of a woman whose extraordinary beauty caused a murmur of admiration to arise as she came in. It was Madame Ghislaine Roberval, the widow of the celebrated inventor who had produced the electric automobile that was driving gasoline cars from the market.

She entered the salon at the precise moment when someone was saying to Gribal:

"Mademoiselle Paulette is making conquests."

"Yes?" he answered, non-committal but flattered.

"Her conversation seems to have drawn to her the most intelligent and fashionable man in Paris. Don't you know him? It's the Marquis de Saint-Imier."

The name struck Gribal like a flash of lightning. He excused himself to seek his daughter, all unsuspicious of the danger she was in. Or was it already too late? Had Paulette already said more than she should?

But the crowd separated him from her. He could only wait, his heart beating rapidly with fright. Saint-Imier was there! The audacity of the man was beyond anything he had imagined. And in spite of himself, Gribal became the witness of a singular scene.

Near him, Ghislaine Roberval was passing by, majestically beautiful followed by Saint-Imier, whose hot eyes burned with an extraordinary fire as he looked after her. The Marquis approached the beautiful widow and said something to her that Gribal could not avoid hearing very clearly: "Will you come tomorrow? I will wait for you." Madame Roberval looked on the Marquis with a contempt she made no effort to conceal: "You're crazy," she said. "You give me the horrors."

She turned her back on the Marquis, leaving him pale with rage. Tenaciously, he maneuvered through the crowded room to regain her attention. But no less obstinately, she fled him, without disguising her dislike and her impatience. It was so pointed that people began to watch them, the more so since the Marquis, for once in his life, seemed to have lost all control of himself.

Finally, at a moment when Saint-Imier was about to rejoin her again, Madame Roberval, without affectation, took the arm of a young man in the adjoining salon. Someone said:

"It's Monsieur Gabriel de Neuville, the young diplomat."

For a moment it looked as though the Marquis would leap on his rival, but he contented himself with giving him a glance of pure hatred, and moving slowly away as though the public snub had not affected him. He even smiled—but with what a smile!

Gribal was able to get to Paulette finally, and to her great astonishment, led her toward the cloakroom.

"Are we going already, father?"

Then she noticed her father's agitation and did not insist. But in the taxi which was taking them back toward the Rue Boissy d'Anglas she did not hide her annoyance:

"What's the trouble? Did I do something wrong? Why did we have to leave so early?"

"No, daughter, what happened is hardly your fault. You don't understand?"

"Understand what?"

"That Marquis, who was talking to you—"

"Well?"

"You had better avoid him, daughter."

"He is not a nice person?"

"No. What did he say to you?"

"He asked me what you thought of the end of the world."

"And you mentioned Mazelier?... And the helium lamp?"

"Yes… Shouldn't I have?"

"No."

"Why?"

"I'll tell you in a moment. But be reassured. You couldn't know. I should have told you not to say anything about it, about anything that happened yesterday. For that matter, I couldn't know that you would meet that man."

"But that man, can he do you any harm?"

Gribal made an evasive gesture.

Paulette was not stupid; her brain was working furiously.

"Then," she said, "I must have touched on a dangerous secret without knowing it?"

"Perhaps."

"This secret—do you know it, father?"

"No."

"Does Professor Mazelier?"

"I don't know. He may know no more than I do."

Paulette did not dare to ask confidences her father was unwilling to give. She said in a meditative voice:

"That man, father, he really frightens me. And his voice… It seems to me that I have heard it somewhere. Ah, if I could only remember."

All at once, she gave a little cry:

"I know, father. I know where I heard it. It was yesterday, on the radio. Therefore, it was he who—"

Gribal took his daughter's hand:

"Hush, Paulette. And above all, don't talk like that to your mother or to Roger."

Was any further doubt possible? Paulette also had identified the man who had threatened the world so madly and shouted his hate for the whole human species over the radio.

66

The cause of this hate? A matter of no importance—the important thing was to defend oneself against the man as against some wild beast, and to bring him down like a mad dog.

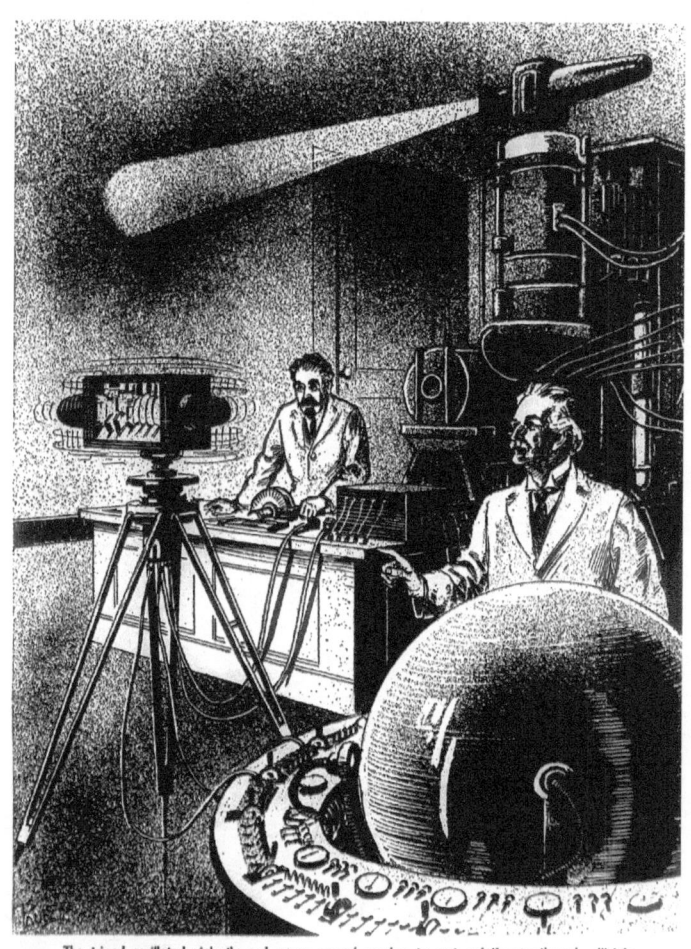

The tripod oscillated violently and swung around coming to rest pointing northward. "M.de Saint-Imier's auto has turned turtle on the Estampes road," Mazelier said quietly.

CHAPTER VII
THE MAID AND THE CHINESE MAN

At the office, where Mazelier and Gribal were discussing the matter in the silence of after-hours, they arrived at a single determination to use any possible means to suppress the adversary who, pretending ignorance of things scientific, nevertheless possessed powers of the first order.

Mazelier repeated for the 16th time: "It's going to be a hard fight."

"Are you discouraged, Professor?" asked Gribal, worried. Mazelier lifted his head: "I will carry on the fight to my last breath," he cried. "I only wanted you to understand that from now on we two are directly threatened."

"What can we do?"

"Nothing. Wait."

After a moment of silence Mazelier added: "Listen, Gribal: if he gets me, you will have to take my place immediately. If you are the first to fall, I will do anything on earth to make him pay for it. Now, I must put you in touch with what means of defense we possess. For we have some—and not so feeble, either. Do you see that sphere? What do you think it is made of?"

Gribal looked at the gleaming ball with its electrical connection and dials which the scientist had used in calculating the center of the emission of the cold and dark waves.

"I don't know that metal," he admitted.

"It is not metal, my friend. It is made of solidified air. I had to experiment a long time before finding a means of producing it. And this globe of solidified air is also, as you have reason to know, an excellent loudspeaker. But it contains a special apparatus which is at one and the same time a radiometer and an emission-generator. It is from the interior of that sphere that the emissions went forth that counteracted those of Saint-Imier. You must learn how to use it, Gribal. But I warn you that it is impossible to use it without producing always some very strange and unpredictable effects."

"Dangerous effects?"

"Sometimes, if one is not careful. In any case, of such force that they would not pass unnoticed. What would you say if at a given moment all the motors in Europe suddenly stopped? All the autos, all the electric railroads, all the subways, everything but steam engines?"

"You could do that?"

"Easily, Gribal. By the use of the same apparatus I could blow up at the same moment all the explosives, all the projectiles and all the other munitions within a given field of radiation. Unfortunately for war use, those nearest would go first! I imagine that I could also act upon the nerves and muscles of living beings. You see why I cannot confide the use of this apparatus to everybody?"

"Professor," said Gribal, stirred, "I will be worthy of your confidence."

"I know it, my friend. But be careful of the consequences of the slightest indiscretion, of the slightest overheard remark. Ask yourself only what would happen if the Marquis de Saint-Imier were aware of the method I have followed. I would have to bend all my efforts to undoing everything I have done. Singular situation!

"With my sphere, I opposed the radiation emitted by Saint-Imier with more powerful emissions. No doubt you noticed that I was worried yesterday. It was because I was not at all sure of the effects of the radiation I discovered. I might very well have intensified the catastrophe instead of preventing it. But I had to risk everything to gain everything. And fortunately it turned out well. In that single hour of combat I learned more than any time in my life."

These reflections had a peculiar effect on Gribal; he had a certain sensation of retrospective fear.

"Ah," he murmured, "what would have happened, if you had not been here?"

Simply and calmly, as though he were delivering a lecture, Mazelier went on: "This is what would have happened. In all the countries under the influence of the radiation emitted by the Marquis de Saint-Imier there would not be a single living being at this moment."

Mazelier went on: "Reynier-Vitral was right. Living beings can exist in an atmosphere composed differently than ours. He is right to remember the precision oxygenators invented by Bayeux. But he was wrong in imagining the phenomenon could have lasted. A frightful poisoning would have finished us all off, not to mention the cold. We would not have been far from the 80 below zero Paulette mentioned."

"But how was it that the phenomena of destruction were localized, if I can put it that way, in the region east of Passy? The Marquis threatened the whole world, and more than half the world escaped. *Parbleu!* I see, though... The Marquis arranged it so that he was outside the effects!"

Mazelier shook his head.

"No, Gribal, don't think that. The dark, the poisoned air, the cold, the destruction of cellular matter would have manifested themselves to the west as well as to the east. It was only a question of minutes."

"But in that case the madman would have shared the fate of his victims!"

"Who knows? Perhaps that madman, as you so justly call him, was anxious to die. He is not the first who has wished that everything should go down when he went."

In his turn, Gribal made a negative gesture:

"Oh, come, Professor! Be reasonable. The man is still young; he is not more than 45, Paulette says. He is rich. He is the center of the Paris fashionable world. He has everything he needs to make him happy. And he wished to die—to die amidst the destruction of the world. It is inadmissible; it is hardly possible that he is as crazy as that."

"That is his secret," replied Mazelier gravely, "and I admit to you that I don't know the reason. It's enough that I know the fact. The man is a danger to humanity; he must be reduced to powerlessness."

"And if he repents some day?"

"Well, Gribal, the Church tells us that we must pardon those who repent. But we must also be pitiless to those who persist in evil."

"Doubtless. But how can I believe that this man wishes to do the same thing as some people I knew at Marseilles?"

"Good," said Mazelier with a laugh, "you're going to tell me some tall story, but go on."

"I swear it is nothing but the truth. You remember that in 1910 there was a good deal of talk about whether Halley's comet would hit the Earth and reduce it to fragments? Well, my Marseilles friends climbed up to the belfry of the cathedral, there to have a better view of the end of the world."

"You're right, at that, my friend, not to take the matter too tragically. Too bad we can't have young Roger with us—he knows how to look at these things."

The name of his son recalled to Gribal that he was keeping his lunch waiting.

"We're going to be late getting to the table," he said, pulling out his watch.

Mazelier, who never knew what time it was, approved.

"Well, let's get something to eat then. Come back right away, Gribal, and we'll get busy on it immediately...Ah, by the way, do you remember that work you did on yttrium, zirconium and tungsten? You remember that you established certain analogies and called them the 'masked bodies?' "

"I remember perfectly, although it was some time ago."

"At the time I gave you my own notes on the subject. You have them still?"

"I should say so. They are locked in my desk along with the most precious of my other papers."

"In that case, I suggest that you bring them back to the laboratory when you come. We are going to need them."

"Nothing easier."

"All right. Goodbye, Gribal."

"Till after lunch, Professor."

Gribal arrived at his home in a state of enthusiasm difficult to describe accurately. The previous worry had fled; he felt only the high spirits of the fighter who has become certain of victory. What he now knew of the labors and discoveries made by Mazelier reassured him completely. Who in the world could equal him? Nobody, he answered himself; Saint-Imier was already beaten, for Mazelier saw into scientific depths to which the other was a stranger.

He leaped up the stairs four at a time. But a surprise was waiting for him; there was no lunch ready. Madame Gribal met him in the entryway:

"Did Suzie come back with you?"

"The maid? Of course not. I haven't seen her."

And perceiving that his wife looked a little worried, he inquired:

"Has she gone out, then?"

"Yes, father," answered Paulette, "and it's so queer! She went out to do the marketing at about 9 a.m."

"And she hasn't come back?"

"You can see. And it's now 12:40 a.m."

Gribal grumbled:

"That's carrying things a little far."

"Something must have happened to her," declared Paulette.

"Oh, I hope she hasn't been run over," said Madame Gribal. "There are so many street accidents nowadays."

Roger, philosophical as ever, offered a more comforting hypothesis:

"Probably gone to a talkie and forgotten what time it was."

His mother replied severely:

"You know very well there aren't any morning talkies anymore."

This delay was really worrisome. Suzie, who was from Brittany, a native of Saint-Guénolé, was a pearl among housemaids. Clever, a hard worker, careful and honest, quick to obey and speaking little, she had been in the employ of the Gribal household for over a year. She never asked for extra evenings out, never had to be reprimanded. She appeared for work with such regularity that the concierge of the apartment was in the habit of saying:

"Ah, that Suzie must have a clock in her middle. You could run a railroad by her."

"What shall we do?" asked Madame Gribal, a prey to somber imaginings.

Gribal was perplexed.

"Faith," he said, "let's wait a little longer. What should I do? If she doesn't show up, I'll report the matter to the police."

And then, to reassure his wife, he added:

"I don't think there has really been any accident. They would have let us know, and she's been gone long enough for them to send word."

But he himself was not really convinced. Meanwhile, he decided to look up the notes of the experiments of which Mazelier had spoken. He knew exactly where they were—a little secret drawer at the back of his desk.

He took out the key for the drawer and—stupefaction! —found it wide open. Hardly believing his eyes, Gribal called:

"Paulette! Have you been in my desk?"

The young girl ran to him:

"Of course not, father. You know very well that no one would touch your—"

She did not finish. Gribal gave a cry of astonishment and annoyance; the secret drawer had been forced; the note books and the package that had contained them were gone.

Roger and his mother, hurrying to the scene of the disturbance, looked in astonishment at the too-evident traces of the robbery. After a moment of silence, Madame Gribal spoke:

"But it's impossible! Impossible!"

"Yes," said Gribal, controlling himself with an effort, "it's impossible, but it happened! Look, has anyone at all been here during my absence?"

"Nobody, absolutely nobody."

"And you didn't go out yourself?"

"Not for a moment."

"Who has been in this room?"

"Suzie. And Suzie alone. She did up the room before going for the food."

"In which room does she usually begin?"

"She usually begins in the dining room instead of this one."

"And which room does she do last?"

Paulette and her mother replied together:

"Your office."

"And she went out immediately afterward?"

"Yes, but—" demanded Madame Gribal, "all the same I hope you don't suspect her."

No, Gribal did not suspect her. All the same there was the evidence. Drawers do not force themselves; papers don't take wing and fly away. Who else could have entered the room?

Most important of all, who would have gained from the crime? Certainly the missing documents were of the greatest importance, since Mazelier had been so urgent about having them at the office. Now, what possible advantage would they be to Suzie, an illiterate servant from Brittany? And who could have told her of the existence of the secret drawer or what it contained?

In any case, no further hesitation seemed necessary; the police must be called in. Gribal clapped on his hat and hurried off to the nearest station, but on the very doorstep remembering Mazelier's counsels of prudence, said nothing of the loss of his papers.

"A servant four hours late?" The affair seemed to the policeman on duty one of the smallest importance. Nevertheless he asked the usual questions, taking notes:

"What was the name of your maid?"

"Suzie Kerdel."

"Ah! A Bretonne?"

"Yes, from Saint-Guénolé."

"Oh, in that case, she will be easy to find. There's a peculiarity about the women of that neighborhood, I know it. They look very Chinese. A skin almost yellow, slanting eyes, long black hair. Doesn't that describe your maid?"

"Perfectly," said Gribal, surprised and strangely moved by the observation, which had never struck him before. *Chinese type*—the idea roused in him curious associations and memories.

"Any special details? How was she dressed when she left your house?"

"As usual; that is, she wore a regular Breton costume."

"That will make the search very much easier. There are not too many of those queer Saint-Guénolé bonnets running around the Paris streets."

"Where did she live?"

"She went home every evening; 43 Rue Faber."

"At Grenelle? Good. I thank you, Monsieur. Go home to your lunch; I promise you that before your next meal you will have news of her."

And the policeman added, with a smile:

"Even if she was 48 that makes no difference. Women can do their running around at any age."

Gribal did not answer, and for a good reason. His suppositions cut considerably deeper than those of the policeman, but they seemed so absurd that he rejected them as untenable.

The most reasonable thing to do at present was to wait for the results of the police inquiry and to warn Mazelier as soon as possible. There was still time to put the police on the track of the stolen notes if the scientist thought the effort would be worthwhile.

Gribal was so much affected by the loss of the notes that he was a little apprehensive about seeing his superior again. The engineer moved toward the office, but emotion seemed to halt his footsteps. The scientist would never believe such a fantastic story—a theft on the very morning when he had asked for the notes! And at the best, he could not but draw the conclusion that Madame Gribal paid very little attention to what went on in her house. It was both ridiculous and painful; in fact, nothing can be worse than the situation of a victim to whom one can say, "It was your fault." As he passed the concierge's lodge, he stuck his head in to ask Père Bibent:

"Has Professor Mazelier come back yet?"

"He went up just before you, Monsieur Gribal."

The engineer sighed. He hated to face it. But he consoled himself with the thought that after all, he had not much with which to reproach himself.

CHAPTER VIII
THE MYSTERIOUS SAINT-IMIER

He encountered the scientist at the door of the inner laboratory.

"Ah, there you are, Gribal! I was afraid I was late and was keeping you waiting. Come along in."

"Professor," babbled the engineer nervously, "I'm sorry to have to tell you that—"

Mazelier, as he was taking off his hat and coat, had looked around with the experienced eye of the methodical worker to see that everything was in its place before beginning. And now suddenly, like Gribal before the forced desk, and while the other was in mid-sentence, the scientist gave a cry of pain, surprise and anger. Then, clutching at his heart, he would have fallen, had not Gribal sustained him and assisted him to a chair.

"Are you ill? I'll open the window"

Clumsy and hurried, like anyone else in such a case, Gribal fumbled with the catch, but was called back by Mazelier:

"Gribal! Look! The sphere... the dials... disappeared!"

The engineer turned, rubbing his eyes, refusing, in his turn to admit the reality. The dials, the connections, the sphere, had all vanished.

Underneath his frail-looking exterior Mazelier concealed more energy and decision than his assistant. He made no complaint, expressed no regret. Recovered from his momentary weakness, as calm as though he were giving directions for some minor experiment, he said:

"Someone has stolen the whole apparatus. Not an hour ago. Let us discover how it was done—if possible."

"Didn't you lock the laboratory door when you went out to lunch?" asked Gribal, restored by his superior's magnificent cool-headedness.

"Yes. I remember it perfectly. Besides I have just opened it again with my key, and in opening, found nothing unusual about the lock. Let's have a look at the window."

It looked out on the Avenue des Champs-Elysées. The laboratory was on the fourth floor, and it was impossible that a thief, in broad daylight, had managed to climb to such a height to get in. Moreover the glass was intact, the catch still closed. Nobody could possibly have touched the window.

"Therefore," said Mazelier in his calm voice, as they ended the examination, "someone got in with a false key. Let's go see Père Bibent. But don't say anything that might frighten him, nor anything that would rouse his suspicions about what happened. I don't want him talking."

Père Bibent himself had one of those honest, rock-hewn faces; Mazelier had known him for too long to suspect the old man himself of such a piece of thievery.

"Tell me, Bibent, did anyone call to see me while I was out?"

"Oh, no, Monsieur."

"I expected someone, and when I went out I clean forgot to tell you. Look, try to remember—you didn't see anyone at all?"

"No, no one asked for you Professor Mazelier, I'd swear. The only person here this noon was a kind of huckster selling little statuettes. A yellow man."

"Ah, a huckster? That's funny; those chaps are black for the most part."

"Ah, if you had been five minutes later going out to lunch you would have seen him as clearly as I did. You had hardly gone out, both of you before he arrived."

"What sort of little statuettes did he have?"

"Oh, ivory ones. I chased him along. He looked like a bad egg with his big mouth and yellow skin and his nose all flattened out. A kind of a Chinese, I tell you, Professor Mazelier."

"A Chinese!" cried Mazelier and Gribal together.

"Yes. I shut the door in his face and didn't see him again. That's all. But aside from that, nobody has been here during the lunch-hour. Sure and certain."

"Thank you, Bibent."

The two men returned to the office. In the laboratory they looked at each other.

"Well, Gribal?"

"Well, Professor, It was probably the Marquis' chauffeur."

"Do you think so?"

"I don't think so, I'm sure of it. But if I can explain what happened here, I am at a loss to explain what happened at my own house."

"At your house?"

"Yes. My desk was forced this morning, and someone took—"

"Someone took?"

"The notes on the experiments, Professor."

The expected words of blame did not come. Instead, Mazelier said simply:

"That does not surprise me, my friend."

And he added, after a minute:

"Never mind those notes. We can write it all up again. I remember them fairly well."

"After ten years?"

"There are certain things one does not forget, Gribal. You will see when we get to it. But I understand how the theft was committed here. Do you know the means at your place?"

"I can only suspect my maid, and I can't believe it was she."

"Have you talked to her?"

"No. She went out this morning to do the marketing. She had not yet come back when I left."

"Well then, Gribal, it was she. She stole the notes and then ran away."

"But that would be so stupid. By this time they have certainly found her. The man at the police station was right. A Bretonne in a Saint-Guénolé bonnet would be easy to find in Paris. Especially since I have her home address."

"Did you say she was from Saint-Guénolé? She must have been a descendant of that colony of Orientals there, in that case"

"She looked quite Chinese, as a matter of fact."

"It was she, Gribal. Decidedly, we have very little luck with the Chinese today."

Was Mazelier quite undisturbed by the double theft, since he found the heart to joke about it? Gribal himself was the prey of a considerable feeling of uneasiness, which he did not seek to conceal from his superior. The marvelous sphere, the machine that had saved humanity from disaster, Mazelier's greatest discovery, was in the hands of the redoubtable enemy of the race, who thus sent his agents everywhere. Would he not make it the instrument of new crimes, perhaps an ultimate disaster?

"Ah, my friend, there never was a more useless burglary! The Chinese man had hardly got out of here before the sphere vanished from his hands. The solidified air of which it was composed became gaseous again. And as to the radiation-generators within it, they are completely gone by this time. The whole apparatus was kept in a state of abnormal equilibrium by radiation emitted by another apparatus within this laboratory—look. Our friend, the Marquis de Saint-Imier has stolen nothing but a mirage, Gribal. And every time he does something like that he leaves another trail pointing to himself of which we can make use. He thinks he has us now, whereas it is we who have him."

"Well, what do we do next then?"

He interrupted himself, prey to a sudden nervousness, and began to pace back and forth in the laboratory.

"You will see, my friend. We will make another solidified air sphere, better and more easily handled than the first. We will get to work on a whole group of new forms of radiation. The atom is going to yield up to us its last secrets. For everything is possible, Gribal. You hear—everything, absolutely. This Saint-Imier is an imbecile, in trying to limit something that has no limits. Doesn't he see that matter cannot be destroyed?"

He halted, thoughtful for a moment. Then he continued his train of thought, speaking, one would say, more for his own benefit than for Gribal's.

"Yes, *parbleu!* The Chinese man slid into the stairway and went up the minute Bibent's head was turned. Yes, the maid at your house had precise instructions. But all that has no real interest. What I would like to know is—yes, yes, the only important detail is how Saint-Imier discovered the existence of the sphere and the notes. He found it all out in the course of a few hours this morning. How in the world did he do it?"

And replying to a question which Gribal had not pronounced, Mazelier went on:

"How did he see what went on here and in Gribal's house?"

That same evening Gribal found at his house a communication from the police. They announced that their inquiry had received a complete setback. Suzie Kerdel remained unfound.

A single significant detail. In the Rue Faber, at the address she had given, no one knew of her. The pearl among maids was, according to all appearances, nothing but a crook. Madame Gribal, ignorant of the whole truth, could not understand. Suzie disappeared? She must have been the victim of gangsters who had first robbed and then killed her, probably thrown the body into the Seine or cut it in pieces and hid it somewhere. The poor woman was really in despair.

As to Paulette, she did not partake of these kindly illusions, but she kept her opinions to herself, and this silence pleased Gribal considerably. He was still more pleased with his daughter when she offered to help her mother with the household duties instead of hiring another servant. "Economy," she said to her mother, and then in her father's ear whispered, "economy—and take no chances."

Gribal understood that although Paulette knew nothing, she had guessed nearly everything, and realized that if things became complicated he had an assistant he could rely upon.

For the moment there were no complications. At the office the work went on as usual, and as though nothing had happened. Mazelier, however, was more careful than usual to let the press and public know about all the work he was carrying on and the results hoped for from it. Nothing to hide, was the key, nothing to hide, and nothing sensational being done. But would these precautions really hide from the Marquis de Saint-Imier the fact that Mazelier and Gribal, in the silence of the inner laboratory, were continuing their secret research?

The Marquis himself was equally open. Apparently he was enormously busy about everything but scientific research. For one thing he was out of the city. The newspapers were full of a big *fête* he was giving at Nice, where he had assembled performers to give a series of all the known dances from all the different parts of the world, ending up with the massed performance of a troupe of 500 dancers in the open air, including the best artists of the Paris stage.

At Pau, he was organizing a series of boxing matches; next he was at Chamonix in the midst of a mountain-climbing expedition. He went over to Algiers and held a camel race, he arrived at Touggourt and played practical jokes on the grave Arab sheiks there. His success at Naples was less striking, his efforts to reproduce the destruction of Pompeii on the scene, having aroused the anger of influential Italian circles.

He was next heard of in London, organizing a race among the "super-horses" of the British Empire, ridden by an assemblage of the best jockeys in the world. In fact, he was living the life of a superman of fashion, throwing money out of all his windows, and as he was as polite as he was generous, as distinguished as he was extravagant, he enjoyed a considerable esteem in his world.

Could one possibly suspect such a person of having conceived a gigantic and savage attempt on the lives of millions, and even more, of having tried to carry it out?

Mazelier and Gribal had almost arrived at the conclusion that they were wrong. The Marquis was surrounded by people, by servants; perhaps one of them, keeping carefully in the background, was the real criminal. It was not at all impossible.

But always they ran up against Paulette's observations: the voice that had come over the radio, and which had been heard by everyone, she remained certain that it was the same voice she had heard in the minister's drawing room. One can be deceived in voices, but she insisted.

One morning, on opening his paper, Gribal noticed a small item in the society column. The Marquis de Saint-Imier was returning to Paris. He was going to give a series of costume balls at his house in the Rue Cortambert. It would attract the whole smart world of Paris; one could not consider oneself in style if one did not receive an invitation.

Meanwhile the days were going by in absolute calm for Gribal and Mazelier. Paris had already forgotten the strange autumn night in the middle of the day; the judicial inquest that had been opened to discover the identity of the "practical joker" had been quickly closed without result. Would Mazelier have time to complete his experiments without any further interference?

One afternoon in March, Mazelier was working in the laboratory at the office. He had sent Gribal to the library to consult Reynier-Vitral's latest work on isotopes; he was in the main laboratory. About him the other research workers were watching an electric furnace in which the scientist was carrying on, with improved apparatus, the experiments of Wöhler and David in the production of synthetic diamonds by means of boron. Mazelier was seated at his desk, busily working out chemical formulas.

All at once he felt his chair move and sway, as though from a powerful earthquake shock. The movement was so violent that Mazelier was thrown from his seat, his head striking the sharp point of a magnetic instrument that he had placed on the desk that very morning. As he fell, the scientist cried out; the others gathered round him and lifted him up half-conscious. Fortunately the wound was insignificant, but a quarter of an inch in either direction and it might easily have been fatal.

The assistants could not understand the accident. They had felt no shock, perceived no movement. In the whole laboratory nothing had moved but Mazelier's big armchair.

"Decidedly, I'm getting clumsy in my old age," the scientist explained when the wound had been treated. "I must have moved too quickly."

He had no more to say on the subject. But he moved the magnetic instrument away and had workmen take from his office every object that possessed dangerous corners. And when Gribal arrived, he took him into the inner laboratory and locked the door. The assistants noticed that Gribal looked worried when he emerged some time later.

Nevertheless, during the following days, everything went along in order. Mazelier carried on his work as usual, without making any further allusions to his accident.

But one morning Gribal, who felt in the most excellent health when he went to bed, woke up with a frightful headache. He took an aspirin, but without the slightest effect. What was worse he felt extremely weak, and even for him to go to the office demanded an effort that took the last bit of his energy. As he got out of the taxi at the door, he crumpled to the sidewalk, and Bibent had to help him upstairs, and as he arrived at the laboratory he fainted.

The scientist was alone in the office at that moment; it was early and the assistants had not yet arrived.

"Shall I call a doctor?" inquired the concierge.

"Yes, yes, hurry up. But before you do that, help me get him into the inner laboratory."

Alone with Gribal, inanimate in the big armchair where he sprawled, Mazelier acted quickly and with certainty. Near the big sphere of brilliant metal on the table, he found a button, touched it, and then pulled a lever. There was the sound of a low humming, a vibration made itself felt, and the hum deepened to the sound of the lowest tone of some great organ. After a minute or two Gribal opened his eyes, then moved in his chair, sat up and said:

"I think I must have fainted."

"You certainly did, my friend. Do you feel better now?"

"I feel quite all right. *Parbleu!* My headache is gone. It was really stupid of me to pass out like that. Something must be wrong with my digestion."

CHAPTER IX
ATTEMPTED MURDER

Mazelier maneuvered another lever and the vibration ceased.

"Ah," said Gribal. "You have been using the sphere."

"Yes, to cure your headache."

"Ah. Indeed. But—"

"But, my dear fellow, you never had headaches like this before."

"I should say not. What happened to me, anyway?"

"You were poisoned, that's all."

"Poisoned!"

"Literally. Poisoned by radiation let loose in your bedroom, where you were quite alone; poisoned by the Marquis, our little friend, who seems to be taking active measures. Your wife didn't have a headache?"

"No; she got up an hour before I did."

"Well, that's what saved her. And if you had not come down to the office—"

Gribal grew pale.

"Will it happen again do you think?"

"We shall see. The other day, I just missed killing myself. This morning you just missed dying. I just managed to save you. But it's all right now. The danger is over."

"For the time being."

"Yes, for the time being. But it was really my fault that you were in danger at all."

"Oh, come."

"Certainly. I've been working in the main laboratory as you know, and so didn't want to have on me the little apparatus with the buzzer that warns of the presence of unknown forms of radiation. That's how it happened the other day that I wasn't warned of the attack on me—or rather, on my chair. And for the same reason, not having one of these revelators at your house, Gribal, you were not warned this morning that you were in danger."

"Doubtless. But how is that your fault?"

"You should have one of these revelators with you all the time. And take Paulette into the secret, too. Your wife and Roger can think that it's some queer kind of watch which strikes the hour. I only hope they don't try to wind it up. And you, whenever you hear it, no matter where you are or for what, go away from there fast. You will be in real danger. And now Gribal, let's get busy. We must make one of these revelators for you; better make another for Paulette."

"But if he invades this laboratory with his radiations?"

"He can't. I have set up a barrage-curtain of counter radiation."

And Mazelier pointed to the sphere:

"There's our defense-machine. Always on the job. Unfortunately, I can't extend the curtain to cover us when we get out of these four walls."

"And won't the Chinese man come back?"

"Certainly not. Oh, for that, he will hardly try; he will know that we will be on guard. But if he does get in, he won't get out again alive. That's why only you and I are permitted to come in here. But wait, Gribal, I must show you; it's possible you will have to get in some day without me. I'll show you how to do it. Look here—"

Mazelier rose and opened the door of the inner laboratory.

"You see the key-hole? And the glass plates above and below? Well, when I go out, I press on this place here, which is attached to the upper plate. Before going in again, I press on the lower place. That's all, but you mustn't forget. Do you understand?"

"I think I see," said the engineer, "pressing on the upper button actuates a curtain of deadly radiation; the second stops the generator and permits one to go in."

"Right, Gribal. And note that the buttons are hidden under the form of the screws that hold the glass plates. I defy Saint-Imier or any of his assistants to find them. But you see—in the whole wide world, we have only this one place that is absolutely safe. But admit that you thought me crazy in doing so much work on the doors of my inner laboratory."

"Professor," said the engineer with a smile, "you know very well that a good soldier obeys without asking questions. We are now engaged in a war; I am a soldier."

"Admirable, my friend. The more so, since like a good soldier you carry out all orders to the letter, even when you don't understand them."

As he spoke, Mazelier had been working over a watch-case, in which he was installing a tiny apparatus.

"Your revelator will be ready tomorrow. I will still have to put something into it which I don't have at the moment. I hope only that I won't be interrupted tonight in my work."

"Do you think he's going to invade your house too?"

"Anywhere, I repeat, he will follow us anywhere."

"But," demanded Gribal suddenly, "can't we send him the same kind of a visiting card?"

Mazelier shook his head.

"Do you think I haven't thought of that? Unfortunately, before I can do that—you see, I might make any number of innocent victims. The apparatus for attack waves, which I have been developing as well as he, is not yet refined enough to enable me to concentrate on a point like that. I must be able to direct the wave action where I wish and they must act nowhere but on that spot."

And Mazelier went on, with a cold fury that astonished his companion:

"On the day I find out how to do that, we can be at rest, for I swear I will not hesitate."

"But he has attack waves, and is not hesitating to use them, whether he can control them or not!"

"Doubtless. But he is a criminal. I wonder how many innocent people he struck down this morning, trying to reach you? Or how many other accidents he caused the other day, trying to cause one for me? Ah, the monster!"

And coming back to the idea that obsessed him, Mazelier went on:

"But how was he able to see? For he did see, Gribal! How did he know the exact placing of my chair and your bed. I must know or lose the game!"

Paulette was not an athletic young woman. Nevertheless she had been an enthusiastic bicyclist since her 15th year, fearless even of the Paris traffic, amid which she maneuvered with an agility and cleverness worthy of a professional. She managed her wheeled steed with a gay carelessness that nearly gave Madame Gribal tremors, but which Roger found the most natural thing in the world.

On this particular day, returning from the university, Paulette realized that she was distracted. People often ask what young girls think about; this one on a bicycle thought about dodging buses, automobiles and pedestrians, not counting the new high-speed "motos" that whizzed through the streets like meteors.

A traffic jam brought Paulette to a halt at the Pont de la Concorde. The Boulevard Saint-Germain, as far back as the Ministry of Foreign Affairs, was packed with vehicles, and the tumult of their horns was infernal. But there was nothing to do but wait till the police untangled the mess. Mechanically Paulette looked around.

All at once, she gave a little "Ah!" of surprise. Quite close to her, separated only by a taxi, a huge auto had halted. Paulette's gaze fell on the chauffeur, who was quite exceptionally unhandsome. Buck teeth, slanting eyes, mouth that reached from ear to ear. Paulette expressed it to herself, "Where in all China did they find him?"

Naturally the young girl's curiosity extended from the chauffeur to the proprietor of the car, and as she looked at him Paulette could not restrain an exclamation of astonishment. She recognized him; it was the Marquis de Saint-Imier. She had seen him only once before and then for hardly five minutes, but she would have recognized him a thousand years after, so forcibly had his features been imprinted on her memory by the circumstances. She looked at him almost fascinated as he lounged among the cushions of his car, disdainful and haughty, not considering the sights of the street worthy of a glance.

Had he seen and recognized Paulette Gribal? It was not at all probable. In any case, there was not a movement, not a change in his face to indicate that he had.

The girl only saw him pick up the end of the speaking tube and give some order to the chauffeur. And then it seemed to Paulette that the chauffeur was looking at her attentively, but out of the corner of his eye. She shivered; then the policeman blew his whistles and the line of vehicles began to trail across the Pont de la Concorde.

As she emerged from the bridge an open space was before her; she had to turn to the left to reach the route to Marly, and prudently looked around. On her right a street-car was coming down the Quai; straight ahead, the autos coming from the other direction were still at some distance; on her left the Cours-la-Reine was quite empty. Paulette turned into the open without the least apprehension.

She had not covered 20 yards when she felt herself suddenly lifted from the ground, turned round and then—It lasted only a split second, but it was like a century, and it was enough for Paulette to recognize that she had been hit from behind by an auto, and that in another fraction of a second she would be rolling with her wrecked bicycle beneath the wheels of the car. She saw herself dying; and then in the third fraction of a second was astonished to find herself on her feet and in the arms of a young man who was asking respectfully:

"Are you hurt, mademoiselle?"

She replied: "Of course not," as though the question had been "Have you a cold?"

Then, suddenly recognizing that she had been miraculously saved from certain death, she cried:

"Oh! Why it's you, Monsieur Duplay."

She was hardly astonished to see him there, for she had met him frequently of late, at her father's office or just near it. Roland Duplay, who had proved a research student of the first order, had been admitted to a considerable degree of intimacy by Gribal. Madame Gribal found him altogether sympathetic, and he had been a caller at the house, where he had told the story of his life's struggle.

His parents had been in business and had sent him to the best technical schools. Then came a change in the family's fortunes, and Roland found himself obliged to abandon his education. He worked; he became an electrician. By means of his labors he procured the funds to buy books and continue that pursuit of pure science which alone could lead him to the fulfillment of his ambitions. And finally his dreams were realized: he had received the powerful protection of Mazelier and Gribal.

His dreams? Perhaps he had other dreams when Paulette shared the lessons which Gribal was giving him. And it was with delight that he had accepted the commission of watching over the girl; from a discreet distance naturally, in a way that she should not suspect. Gribal was anxious; Mazelier had told him to expect anything at all from the Marquis. They had been right. But Saint-Imier did not even know of Duplay's existence.

Paulette, on her part, found it neither surprising nor disagreeable that he should be on hand. "Your poor bicycle," said Roland. "It's in fragments."

The news had a singular effect on Paulette. For the first time she became fully conscious of the fact that it was by a miracle that she had escaped being crushed under the auto, and in the same moment remembered that before the shock, she had recognized the Chinese at the wheel. And if Duplay had not been on hand to catch her, she would have gone under the wheels. She experienced a shiver of retrospective terror.

Nevertheless, she gathered herself together, not wishing her mother to know how narrow an escape she had. To get home now, that was her only desire.

Roland Duplay guessed at her desire. As the crowd of curious persons began to collect and the policeman on duty advanced, thumbing his notebook, the pair were already on their way up the street leading to the Champs-Elysées, and beyond the reach of official inquiry.

They went rapidly as far as the Crystal Palace. There, seated on a park bench where no one would pay any attention to them, they consulted.

Roland was overwhelmed.

"You're more scared than I am!" accused Paulette.

"I admit it."

"Nevertheless, that didn't keep you from saving my life. You pulled me to the left just as I was toppling under the wheels of that car."

"I was lucky enough to be there in time," said the young workman, blushing.

"Tell me, did you have the impression that the accident was…on purpose?"

Roland murmured:

"It isn't an impression; it's a certainty."

"Then that man is a criminal."

Roland did not answer. But he made an affirmative movement with his head.

"What have I done that he should hate me and wish to kill me? Do you know?"

"It isn't because of you yourself. He's aiming at your father and Professor Mazelier."

"But why?"

Roland spoke out clearly:

"Because that man is afraid of them. And he's afraid of them because they are stronger than he is."

All at once Paulette perceived something. Her father had bound her to secrecy on the subject of the incidents at the ministerial reception. Now, Roland Duplay evidently knew both the name of the Marquis and the part he was playing in the drama in which all of them were engaged. But how had he acquired this information?

In answer to her question, the young man did not hesitate to tell her the story of the day of darkness.

"Good," said Paulette, when he had finished, "then we are accomplices."

She was no longer frightened. A combat was begun, and she was now as much engaged in it as anyone; it amused her to think of herself as a soldier. And moreover, she realized that she had a friend and helper in Roland. She held out her hand to him.

"Thank you a thousand times. Till tomorrow, then?"

"I will try to come. Monsieur Gribal is so good to me."

"And you also, you have been good to me. Come tomorrow, and you will see what beautiful lies I can tell. Naturally I don't want mother to know anything about this, she would worry too much. But father, that's something else again. I'll tell him first thing!"

Paulette, entering the house, had her explanation ready:

"Mother!" she cried with all the gaiety with which one would announce a piece of very good news, "do you know, I've lost my bike,"

"Oh yes, I knew you'd forget it someday," said Madame Gribal.

"But I think someone must have stolen it."

Madame Gribal could not avoid noticing the exuberance of her daughter, her rapid and joyous gestures, as though she were possessed of some happy secret.

"My word," she said, "anyone would think it was a pleasure for you to lose it."

This simple observation left Paulette a little confused; she did not know what to answer. But Roger, without realizing it, saved her face for her:

"She ought to be happy about it, mother. If someone swiped that old bike of hers, she'll have to have a new one."

But Paulette was blushing, for she had discovered the cause of her joyous feeling. It was because the loss of the bicycle had been compensated by the gain of an admirer.

CHAPTER X
THEY TRY A DISGUISE

The next morning, Gribal, who had been informed of the details of the adventure through which his daughter had passed, recounted them to Mazelier. The scientist, when he himself was the object of attack, was accustomed to oppose an unruffled calm to the frown of Fate. But this time he gave full rein to his anger. Their opponent had descended to attacks on young girls—nothing equaled the atrocity of such an attempt except perhaps its cowardice.

"I wonder what one would find in the past of this man if we could pry into it. Well, we must get busy, Gribal. I have been delaying too long. Let us attack from our side."

Mazelier was really furious. Let the Marquis attack him if he wished, him an old man, and without family—that was a matter of no importance. When Gribal became an object of attack, it was already a little too much. But Paulette, so intelligent and so cheerful, who seemed destined one day to be a genuine collaborator in the research of the laboratory; Paulette, in the springtime of her life, who deserved so clearly to be happy; Paulette, whom Mazelier loved like one of his own daughters—that was intolerable! The punishment ought to be made to follow the crime with the rapidity of lightning.

"I can strike," said Mazelier, "and I will strike."

But one had to be sure of one's blow. And another difficulty—Mazelier stoutly refused to take any step that might make innocent victims. The forms of radiation he was about to liberate must be made to go straight to their target with the precision of a bullet aimed by an expert marksman. For all those who were even touched by these terrible rays would never recover, even from the simple contact.

"First we must try to find out where we can most easily strike at the animal. Then, Gribal, we will go for him, taking precautions which I trust will be sufficient. I will punish him without remorse, but I would never forgive myself if I made other victims."

"Not even the chauffeur?"

Mazelier hesitated:

"He's only an instrument," he offered.

"Oh, come. He's an accomplice. Saint-Imier gave him the order to run down Paulette, but the chauffeur did not hesitate to do it."

"You are right," said Mazelier reflectively. He went on: "What would you say if we could strike them together?"

"That it would be justice. But how are you going to do it?"

"Look. We don't know anything about the interior arrangements at the Marquis' house. In what room does he live? Where is his secret laboratory, the place where he has perhaps discovered new laws in physics of which I am ignorant? Where does he sleep? We can't do anything against him, under the conditions, without striking at some poor folks around him who are in ignorance of what their master is doing."

"Evidently."

"But suppose—yes, suppose that Saint-Imier gets into his car, driven by that horrible chauffeur. If we could be certain that at a given moment he would pass a certain point, I believe, Gribal, that we could do justice to him. Look, that idea is much more practical than the one of getting at him where he lives; much better than my previous project."

"What was your previous project, Professor?" inquired Gribal, curiously.

"I was going to direct against him radiation that has a terrible effect. They cause the flesh itself to rot, by disintegrating the cellular structure, but the individual subjected to them would doubtless live on for several weeks, the prey of the most acute agonies. They do not kill, you understand; on the contrary, they cause the processes of life to be speeded up. But while the individual who is subjected to them seems to be in the most excellent health, his body is rotting until the day when he becomes nothing more than a skeleton covered with skin. Then—"

"But this radiation," murmured Gribal, "doesn't the Marquis know about its effects?"

"No, my friend. He certainly does not know about this form. For if he did, we would now be rotting, both of us. No, this form of radiation is known to me alone. And you wish to know how I know their effects. Well, do you remember Sully Tavernier?"

"That young pupil of Henri Poincaré, with so much talent, who committed suicide after disappearing from Paris so mysteriously?"

"Poor Tavernier! It was he who discovered this form of radiation, Gribal, by chance, in the course of an experiment—and they bit him. He suffered frightfully— even beyond the limits which imagination can give to pain. He told me about the discovery that was killing him, making me promise never to make the secret public. And then he made his young wife shoot him through the head. She did it, for pity's sake—and then she went insane, Gribal."

"Horrible. My God!"

"What would you have?" said Mazelier, melancholically. "That's the risk we all take in this kind of research. Well, anyway, you see what I was going to do. For this Tavernier radiation, with my apparatus I can project it to a distance, and I hope, concentrate it on a point. But I doubt whether I could do it without striking innocent people, and that is a thing I will never do."

"And I approved," declared Gribal, "but what do you intend to do now?"

"To apply the *lex talionis,*" answered the scientist. "He tried to kill Paulette through an auto accident; well, we will give him an auto accident. And we will see whether he escapes as easily as your daughter."

There was a moment's silence between the two, interrupted by a remark from Gribal: "May I make a request?"

"What is it?"

"If I understand you correctly, you intend to wreck the Marquis' car while it is going at full speed."

"Something like that, Gribal."

"And you can produce the accident from here, seated in your chair?"

"Certainly."

"Without the slightest risk?"

"Without the slightest."

"Well then, let me do it instead of you."

Mazelier gave him a sudden glance of illumination.

"I understand, Gribal," he said. "Yes, the idea which you did not formulate in words has come to me too. I am fighting a scoundrel by rather *scoundrely* means. And you think that I, Mazelier, who has nothing on his old conscience, ought not to descend to the level of a criminal, even to chastise a crime; you fear the effect on my tender sensibilities. Have I guessed it?"

"Professor, I think it is our duty to bring down this bandit. But since we cannot do it in public and under the forms of law and honesty, I beg you to let me take your place. It would be unworthy of you but my position is different; I can take the responsibility. I am the father of the child he tried to kill; that gives me rights you do not possess. And besides, if it comes out, I am only Gribal. While you, you are Mazelier! Your name must remain irreproachable."

The scientist shrugged his shoulders.

"You talk like a boy, my friend. Your scruples are very fine and even refined, but I avow that I see nothing in them whatever. You yourself have made the point that my name is irreproachable. And do you think that an irreproachable man would be so easily dishonored by employing against a man capable of any crime the only means that would really bring him to book? Run along, Gribal, go to the police station and make a formal complaint against Saint-Imier for having tried to assassinate your daughter, and see whether the complaint will not be turned against you. You were speaking of justice a few minutes ago; well, go try the official means of justice. The Marquis will be delighted, I assure you!"

Gribal felt the force of his remarks. But in spite of them, he hesitated, and Mazelier perceived it. The scientist went on, interested by this exaggerated case of tender conscience.

"My friend, remember that it is a case of life and death, not only for us two, but for your family. Remember that I would prefer, like you, to take the matter up with the authorities, and that I would not hesitate for a moment to denounce the Marquis, if it were not evident in a hundred ways that in doing it, I would be playing right into his hands."

"Yes," said Gribal. "I suppose I should not make so much talk about the means chosen to shoot a mad dog. The Marquis, if he is not outside the law, is at least outside humanity."

"Why certainly! The only thing we can do is level all our artillery against him. And that brings up some problems."

"Yes. We must know, first, when the Marquis will make a long trip in his car; second, what road he will take, and third, what time he will leave, his probable speed and the probable moment he will reach the chosen point. Right?"

"You have stated the problem admirably. But one of the pieces of information we already have, to wit, the speed of the car. The Marquis always travels at 50 miles an hour on the open road. His chauffeur is really very skillful. Monsieur Perignon, who has traveled with him not a few times, has informed me on that point."

"Good. But how are we to find out the rest?"

Mazelier was embarrassed. All at once Gribal saw him run to the window of the laboratory which looked out on the Rue de la Boëtie and fling it wide open. A sonorous voice floated up from the street:

"Ol' clo's! I cash ol' clo's."

Mazelier leaned out.

"Hey, there!"

The old clothes merchant lifted his head. Mazelier motioned to him to come up.

"What!" Gribal exclaimed, stupefied, "are you going to sell some clothes?"

Mazelier laughed:

"Just the opposite! I'm going to buy."

The engineer, curious though he was, did not dare to ask questions before the old clothes man who had now entered the laboratory, a pile of hats on his head, and the picturesque cloak of old garments flung over his shoulder.

"Wanna sell something?" he asked, a trifle suspiciously, gazing around the laboratory open-mouthed.

Mazelier was so self-effacing, his natural air was so modest, that the merchant selected Gribal, tall, strong and with the visage of a leader, as the man to whom he should address himself. But Gribal said not a word. He looked toward Mazelier, who began:

"We haven't anything to sell you. But we might like to buy."

"But," objected the merchant, "I haven't anything new."

"Exactly. What we want are some second-hand clothes. Let's see what you've got."

The man spread out his packet, his face lighting at the prospect of doing business, There were workmen's smocks, ragged and stained with rain; old trousers which no doubt knew by heart the names of all the streets of Paris; a few dirty old collars, ties without energy or prestige, and a few other articles that he had the nerve to offer, in his regular patter, as "the very latest models from the fashionable houses on the Boulevard."

Mazelier picked here and there among them, regarding each garment attentively, and calmly offered half the price the man demanded. The offer, after a moment's haggling, was accepted. The seller left, convinced that he was dealing with two men who were quite utterly insane, and promising himself to come back at the earliest occasion to take fuller advantage of their lunacy.

At last, Gribal was free to ask:

"What the Devil do you mean to do with that truck?"

"Try them on, of course! I hope they will fit us."

"What! You want—"

"Yes. I want you to go with me for a little walk near the Rue Cortambert. And for such a walk, it would hardly be a good thing to dress in new morning coats. Look, this ought to be about your size."

"It's frightfully dirty," said Gribal with a shudder. "Well, since we have to…"

"Ah, you understand?"

"I think so. We'll have to dirty ourselves up a bit."

"I assure you that it is indispensable."

When their curious toilet was done, Gribal gave a cry of astonishment to which Mazelier replied with a satisfied grunt. They were completely unrecognizable.

"What in the world do we look like, anyway?" inquired the engineer, more amused than disturbed by the adventure.

"We ought to look like what we are," said the scientist, "that is, a pair of bookkeepers out of work. We're dirty, but respectable. It's a terrible thing not to have a job! Well, let's go eat all the same."

"In the Rue Cortambert?"

"Where else? I noticed a little restaurant there. All the chauffeurs of the quarter take their meals at it. The roast beef must be something wonderful."

"Is it near the Marquis' house?"

Mazelier dropped the joking tone in which he had been speaking:

"It's right across the street."

"We'll be in the lion's jaws."

"Yes, but they won't close on us. He'll never imagine we are so close."

"All right," said Gribal, with another glance at his companion. "We certainly look like a fine pair of birds. We mustn't let Père Bibent see us like this, though. Our reputation would be ruined."

Mazelier shrugged his shoulders:

"Decidedly, Gribal, you would never do for a conspirator! Come along and take your first lesson in camouflage."

"Ah!" said Gribal, in enthusiasm, "you are the limit, my dear Professor. I never imagined that you were such a Sherlock Holmes!"

Mazelier made no reply to this compliment, but opened a little cabinet in the corner of the laboratory where various chemicals were kept, for the most part alkaloids newly developed and still under investigation. From this group of choice poisons, the scientist chose a little bottle:

"Listen, Gribal, we ought to perfume ourselves a little. That will make up for the lack of clean linens. What do you say to this attar of roses?"

Uncorking the bottle, Mazelier held it under Gribal's nose, then sniffed at it himself.

"*Parbleu!*" said the engineer, "I would say that your attar of roses smelled rather more like a fish that had been around for some time. Eh! But my voice has changed. What a curious impression. I don't recognize myself anymore."

Mazelier replied, in a voice equally unrecognizable:

"Isn't that a swell perfume—capable of changing a bass into a soprano with a turn of the hand? Our larynxes will keep the impression for a couple of hours at least. All ready, Gribal?"

"Let's go, Professor Mazelier."

As they passed Bibent's lodge, the old man's head popped out:

"Where are you going?" he asked.

"We're translators. Official diplomas. And we're looking for some work," offered Mazelier.

"But there isn't any in this madhouse of yours," added Gribal.

"Yeah? Well run along and do your translating before I give you something you won't be able to translate," answered the concierge angrily. "Translators, indeed, with pants like that!"

"Well?" inquired Mazelier, when they had attained the avenue.

"Wonderful! The experiment is a success. Too bad we haven't more time; I'd take a run home to see whether they recognized me there. What a voice you have given me, Professor! The voice of a siren—but the siren of a tugboat!"

"And me? Would you recognize this rattle?"

Gribal was filled with confidence. At last, the long nightmare of terror was about to have an end. Nobody would have to worry any longer about the threats of the strange bandit whose social position rendered him so immune to the ordinary methods of attack. Mazelier was right; he would have to be struck as with the hammer of God, unforeseen, almost treacherously, and without pity.

CHAPTER XI
EXPOSED!

The engineer and the scientist were seated before a table in the little restaurant in the Rue Cortambert, looking at the dinner usually given to clients who had large appetites and small purses. They honored the repast without repugnance. They were silent, maintaining the air of men intimidated and humbled by fate. Gribal had his back to the window, and could see, in a mirror facing him, a little of what was going on in the street outside; Mazelier was so placed as to miss nothing of what went on in front of the Saint-Imier mansion.

Such a vigil was capable of lasting a long time without producing any particular result. But Mazelier was patient. He felt sure he would sooner or later make the acquaintance of some member of Saint-Imier's staff and draw interesting information. Neither he nor Gribal had the slightest fear of recognition. Only Saint-Imier himself might possibly be capable of penetrating their disguise, but certainly he would never set foot in such a restaurant.

"This is a good place," said Mazelier aloud for the benefit of the others around them. "We ought to come here again. Ah, if we could only find a job in this section of the town!"

"We can try," said Gribal, entering into the spirit of the occasion.

And in the high, sharp voice which he now used without effort, he added:

"You, you're a stenographer; you ought to be able to find a job in some big house around here."

A chubby-looking chauffeur at an adjoining table, overhearing the remark, as he was intended to, glanced them over rapidly with the penetrating eye of the Parisian workman who can so quickly take the measure of a man. His examination apparently had a favorable result; Mazelier particularly made upon him the impression of a good old chap who was bearing up with dignity under undeserved misfortune.

Poor old man! His shoulders were rounded, his chest pinched, his thin face, cracked and rattling voice, bore the marks of incipient tuberculosis. He was evidently incapable of such feats as piloting a taxi from Montmartre to Vaugirard without missing a single turn or drawing a rebuke from a policeman.

The chubby chauffeur turned a protective glance on Mazelier: "Well, what's the matter, things not so good?" he asked in a sympathetic tone.

"They could be better," Mazelier avowed.

"No use kicking, though," said Gribal, adding after a moment: "Just the same, it isn't because we don't want to work."

"Nor because you don't want to eat either," observed the chauffeur, with a burst of laughter.

"True for you," answered Gribal.

"Certainly," said the chauffeur, "what do they take us for anyway—cows that can eat straw? That's always the way. But what do you do when you have anything to do?"

"We are bookkeepers," replied Mazelier.

"Yes," agreed Gribal, "but we were even better than that at one time, weren't we Martin?"

Mazelier understood that the name of Martin fitted him like the paper on the wall.

"Ah!" he sighed, "much better. When I remember that I was once the stenographer for the Chamber of Deputies—"

The chauffeur opened his eyes to their full extent:

"Not really? And the deputies, they let you go unemployed like this? That's not decent. I know a little about them on my own hook, me. That astonishes you, no? But I know how to speak in public. When the elections come around, the deputy from our district is right on my trail asking me to help him every time. And when I go to see him and ask him for some little favor, you know what he does? Lets me gather moss waiting in his outer office!"

He emptied his glass with a noble gesture and went on: "You look all right, Monsieur Martin. If you'd like me to, I'll look around for something for you."

"Get back my job at the Chamber, for example? I've grown older since those days."

"Of course. Of course. I understand, the old hand isn't as supple—I suppose one has to go like lightning to keep up with the remarks of those johnnies. But, as your friend was mentioning a minute back, you could still hold a job in one of these houses around here."

"Oh yes, I think he could do that all right," replied Gribal.

The chauffeur regarded Mazelier with a sagacious air:

"You must have an education, now? Yes, I know, you know how to do almost anything except find a job. I know. I have a cousin who is taking a course in pharmacy, and he hasn't found a job yet. He'd have died of hunger long ago, if he hadn't got him a job on the railroad. And he's really educated, too; he knows the names of more than 50 laxatives. And he can reel them off in Latin!"

Mazelier gravely lifted his head: "That's wonderful," he approved.

"Yes, but what use is it to him? Well, it's not quite the same thing with you is it? Well, I'll see—you're looking for a secretary's job, in some fashionable house, huh? I know quite a few people in the fashionable world, me. Secretary to a dancer from the Opera, that would hardly do. You're not well enough turned out—oh, nothing personal you understand. I'll find it though. You see."

Mazelier was only giving a minimum of attention to the rambling assurances of his new-found protector. All at once the chauffeur began to gesticulate, lifting his arms in the air.

"Hey! Over here. Come on over, you, I want to say something to you."

A woman had just entered the restaurant and was threading her way among the tables toward the bar. Gribal turned his head mechanically to see the newcomer, and then became as petrified as though he had seen Medusa and both her sisters. It was not the Medusa who was ordering a vermouth-cassis at the bar; the woman in the Breton bonnet had nothing terrifying in her aspect. But Gribal recognized the former maid, Suzie Kerdel!

"Hey, you from Brittany," called the chauffeur, "bring your drink over here, and we'll buy you another one if you're nice."

And when the Bretonne, enchanted with the offer, brought her glass over and seated herself by the chauffeur, the latter continued: "We'll even buy you a couple, if you'll help us out."

Gribal kicked Mazelier significantly under the table. But he might have spared himself the trouble; the scientist had recognized at once the woman for whom the police had searched in vain.

The situation was becoming more complicated than the engineer had foreseen. He busied himself with his plate, and Mazelier imitated him. Would their rashness be turned on them after all? What would happen if the Bretonne recognized them and announced their real station in life in that rough crowd?

Suzie began by swallowing her vermouth-cassis in a single gulp. Then she said: "Ah, but I'm in a hurry today, I must pack the trunks for this evening."

"Your boss going away?"

"I'll say so! Leaving this evening for Biarritz."

"With the Chinese?"

"Who else would he go with?"

"Of course, of course. Well, one has to admit it; there are damn few chauffeurs like that one. He knows how to handle a wheel. Biarritz, you say? He'll make it in eight hours."

"That," said Suzie, "is their business. Is that all you got me over here for?"

And she glanced at her empty glass. The chauffeur understood.

"What will you have with us, little one?"

"Oh, a snifter of curaçao to start with," said Suzie.

Gribal, dumbfounded, did not move. Mazelier tried to keep his self-possession by cutting up a piece of meat into tiny morsels with great care. Suzie paid no attention to them. She went on:

"What was it you were going to ask me? Hurry up; I tell you I've got to get away."

The chauffeur pointed to Mazelier, who, keeping up his role, replied: "It's about me, Madame, if you would be so good—"

"If I would be so good—?"

He played to perfection the part of one of those timid old people always asking for help, but always hesitating and bashful about asking.

"This good man has a regular education," declared the chauffeur, with authority. "Would you consider speaking to your boss about him? You have been there long enough, he ought to have some confidence in you. And he is rich enough to hire a good secretary."

"A secretary?"

"Yes, someone who will do his letters for him. Your Marquis writes plenty of letters, doesn't he?"

"That is, he has someone write them for him," observed Suzie.

"Exactly. Rich people like that don't do anything for themselves. Well, you'll do it then? You'll speak for Monsieur Martin?"

Suzie repeated slowly:

"Monsieur Martin?"

"I live in the Rue d'Arcole," declared Mazelier.

"Good. Write it for me on a piece of paper, will you? When Monsieur comes back from Biarritz I'll bring it to his attention."

The chauffeur threw a triumphant wink in Mazelier's direction:

"Well, old man," he said familiarly, "you see how it works?"

Martin was so much touched that he brushed away a tear.

"Ah, Madame," he cried effusively, "what will you have to drink?"

It was the best means of thanking her.

"This time it will be a little cognac," replied Suzie.

Gribal stifled an exclamation of horror and surprise. This was his model servant, so faithful, so punctual, so temperate, who only rarely, and upon being urged, accepted a little beer or cold tea at his house. What an actress she had been while preparing the way for her theft.

And what was still more incredible, but undoubtedly true, she had not the air of having recognized her former employer.

All at once Suzie looked at Mazelier and began to laugh. The scientist and the engineer were shaken with a single shiver of terror.

"Fortunately," said the Bretonne, "you want a job as a steno and not a singer. Because you have a voice that would kill mice. When I get you the job at our house, don't come into the kitchen. The sound of that voice would curdle the milk."

And she rose to go. The chauffeur still plied her with questions:

"You won't have time to say anything to the Marquis right away, now that Martin is here?"

"Oh, I couldn't do a thing for two weeks yet," said Suzie. "Monsieur is leaving at 9 p.m. And it's already 6:45. I must go. So long!"

"So long, my dear," replied the chauffeur, gallantly. Mazelier, in a tone of emotion, tried to express the depth of his gratitude.

"Madame, I am your servant for life."

"What a lovely remark, and what a musical voice," laughed Suzie.

And she added: "I know. When someone gets married they can have you sing serenades."

And she left on this note of mild pleasantry, to the great relief of her former employer, who had never believed himself well disguised.

Three quarters of an hour later, Mazelier and Gribal were back at the office. As their normal voices had returned, they had only to sing out as they entered:

"Good evening, Père Bibent!"

And the good fellow replied:

"Good evening, Professor Mazelier. Good evening, Monsieur Gribal."

He did not come out of his lodge to watch them go up, unsuspecting the singular spectacle he had missed. But ten minutes later the engineer and the scientist, dressed in their normal fashion, were ready to meet any eye."

"Do you know?" said Gribal, "I was uncomfortable."

"True," said Mazelier pensively, "I had hardly foreseen such an encounter."

"And the chauffeur who mixed in our affairs to get us the protection of that female, that drunkard. And me, I confided the keys of my cellar to her!"

"Did she ever take anything?"

"*Parbleu*, no! She stole nothing but my documents. But there is no longer any doubt possible, she is one of the Marquis' creatures. The important thing is that she did not recognize us."

"Are you certain?"

"What!" cried Gribal, to whom that simple question was like a draft of ice-water on his enthusiasm, "you think that—"

"My friend, I think that woman was quite capable of acting a part for 15 minutes, after having acted one for a year."

"True," said Gribal, discouraged. "But what shall we do?"

"Do the impossible," replied Mazelier.

At the same moment the bell of the door rang.

"Who's calling on us at this hour?" said Gribal. "Don't get up Professor. I'll see."

"Be careful."

"No fear."

A moment later Gribal was back.

"It was only Père Bibent," he announced. "He brought up a note that someone left to be delivered to you."

And Gribal held out an envelope with Mazelier's address upon it. The other tore it open:

"Doubtless a card—ha! Gribal, it was he! Read, read what he wrote."

And he held out to his companion a correspondence card upon which beneath the Saint-Imier coat of arms, appeared in a handwriting, at once elegant and vigorous the following words:

Monsieur Martin may rest assured that I will find a situation for him in which he will be treated as he deserves.

For the first time the Marquis had threatened Mazelier directly and in person. The masks were down; the two adversaries now in open combat.

This bothered Gribal, who was, moreover, affected by so rapid a check to their little plan. But the scientist remained calm.

"*Parbleu!*" he said, "really I like that better. You can no longer reproach me with wishing to stab him in the back. Our clumsiness, or rather our rashness, has brought a good result after all."

"You will not abandon the attempt?"

"Less than ever. The Marquis tried a collective crime against the world; it did not succeed, but the fact remains that he tried, and this gives anyone in the human species the right to suppress him. Moreover, he has committed against you, two crimes under the common law: he stole something from you, and he tried to kill your daughter. This gives us the right—no, this confers upon us the duty, to defend ourselves. And the best defense is an attack."

"But he'll be on his guard now, won't he?"

"I don't think he'll believe we are going to make an attack on him during his journey, and that's just what we are going to do."

"And if he goes by another route?"

"We will know it."

"But we can't follow him."

"I beg your pardon. Without leaving this office, we will take up his trail. For the first time, I am going to apply my newest apparatus; that for which he stole the notes, to a particular case. It's about 8 p.m. now, isn't it? At 9:45, Gribal, turn this little lever here to the left, two centimeters on the scale. That will do the job."

As he spoke, Mazelier indicated one of the maze of attachments leading off from the enormous sphere which replaced the one the Chinese had gotten away with.

"Now, let's get things in order," the scientist went on. "I must direct the concentration of radiation exactly on the point selected, insulate them during their journey, and halt them exactly at the point."

"Can you do it?"

"I hope so."

118

CHAPTER XII
TO BIARRITZ

Before the sphere on the table Mazelier set up a tripod upon which he mounted a box like a small self-contained radio receiving apparatus. But instead of the usual installation, with its bulbs, rheostat, condensers, the box contained nothing but a complex of prisms set at varying angles and a multiplex of lead-sheathed wires. Prisms and wires were detached and re-attached in different combinations, finally appearing at the base of the box in order of size, while on the table before them other prisms were connected up in the opposite order.

"You know, Gribal, that invisible and unsuspected forms of radiation can, when concentrated, upset and confound everything that has been known, up to the present, as a law of nature. Since I have been experimenting in this field, I have become convinced that the so-called natural laws have no real existence. Does that scandalize you?"

"Yes, it does, I admit it. But you have already convinced me laws of nature are nothing but convenient conventions which give us some ground to work from while we are roaming in the prodigious field of phenomena nature presents."

"Right! One must admit that radiation has an existence of its own; the rays have caprices, angers, individual tastes and sympathies. They behave as they like; they do whatever they wish, and to use them one has only to find their preferences. They are comparable to certain people sitting down to dinner, who only eat the dishes they like. Now let's see whether I have succeeded in pleasing this lot. At least I have neglected nothing that ought to please them."

Mazelier closed the box, and attached to its cover another tripod with long sharp points. Then, he carefully turned the whole apparatus this way and that, pointing it in the direction of the Rue Cortambert with the aid of a map of Paris. Finally, he regulated one of the dials placed before the sphere.

"What time is it, Gribal?"

"Exactly 8:30 p.m."

"Good. We have plenty of time. Nothing will happen before 9."

"You think that the Marquis will stick to his program of going out this evening?"

"I am altogether persuaded that the Marquis will think me incapable not only of preventing, but even of defending myself against his attacks at present."

"Just the same he ought to remember that you have escaped him up to now."

"Yes, but his dispositions were not well taken, his apparatus far from complete. Even without my intervention something happened to upset his calculations. But remember what he accomplished that day last October. It was really prodigious."

"What! You still believe that that man is a genuine scientist?"

"Yes, and a scientist of genius."

"You astonish me. I take him for one of those clever amateurs like those courtly gentlemen who studied the structure of the atom under the Cardinal de Rohan in the time of Louis XVI while they were hunting for the philosopher's stone. But a genius—I rather doubt it. But tell me, about that note he sent you—?"

"Oh, I deserved that crack, my dear Gribal."

"All right, I don't want to argue with you about it. Anyhow, it's a declaration of war."

"It would seem like that."

"Then why is he running away to Biarritz after having threatened you?"

"And who told you he was running away? What time is it now?"

"8:55."

"It's time."

Mazelier pressed a button at the base of the box he hid set up and bent over it, listening.

"Nothing yet. Wait a minute. Let me take your watch, Gribal. I am the limit; I completely forgot to wind up my own. Thanks. 8:56, 7... Ah, listen. The Marquis' chauffeur is starting up his motor."

A sort of soft purring, like the sound of water boiling in a teakettle, came from the great sphere.

"Do you hear?" inquired Mazelier, who could not conceal his nervousness. "Now watch my direction indicator. There, Gribal, the tripod on the box. It is suspended so that it can make a complete turn. Automatic, Gribal, it's automatic. Look, it's swinging to the left. Good—now a little to the right. Look, look, what a sharp swing to the right. The Marquis must be about passing the Palais-Royal. What did I tell you? We can follow him wherever he goes. Ah, see, the tripod is pointing to the south. The Marquis' car is headed for the Porte d'Orléans. He must be going to take the Estampes road. Good, good. Now he's slowing up. Ah, he's opened her up again, always in the same direction. Look, the dial indicates 30 kilometers and it's only been 15 minutes. We'll have to act sooner than we thought."

The purring from the sphere continued, synchronously, one would have sworn, with the sound of a big motor, powerful and regular. The direction indicator no longer wavered. It seemed to Gribal that he could hear the beating of his heart answered from the center of the shining sphere. What he was seeing, here in the midst of Paris, in the laboratory of a government establishment, did it not resemble some scene out of a book of medieval magic?

Mazelier no longer busied himself over anything but the slow flight of the hands on the face of Gribal's watch. All at once, he cried out:

"Ready with the lever, there. I'm going to count to ten. At the tenth count, swing it to the left. One…Two…Three…"

The seconds went past with a desperate slowness; an effort of will-power was necessary for him to restrain himself from throwing the lever before the signal. After a century, it arrived.

"Ten!" said Mazelier.

Gribal swung the lever. And suddenly the sphere was silent; the tripod oscillated violently from left to right, then swung completely around and came to rest, pointing northward.

Pale with emotion, Gribal, not daring to say a word, held his breath. Mazelier, also, was paler than usual. But he consulted dial and sphere, and then in his grave, quiet scientist's voice, indifferent to the emotions that were stirring the engineer, he said:

"Monsieur de Saint-Imier's auto has turned over on the Estampes road, 50 kilometers from Paris." And he added tranquilly: "Let's go along to bed, Gribal. Tomorrow morning the newspapers will tell us the rest."

On the next morning, as a matter of fact, nearly all the papers had on the first page an account of the mysterious accident that had occurred on the Estampes road, near Chamarande. But after he had read the story, Gribal rubbed his eyes and then read it again, and leaped from his breakfast table to run to the office where he would find Mazelier. The account ended in this fashion:

One of the most striking personalities in the fashionable world of Paris, especially well known in artistic circles, the Marquis de Saint-Imier, was the victim of an inexplicable accident last evening. The Marquis de Saint-Imier had left Paris at 9 p.m. to go to Biarritz in his car, which was driven by his chauffeur, the Indo-Chinese Pou-Hi, an experienced driver who has been in his service for some time. While traveling at high speed near Chamarande on the Estampes road, about 50 kilometers from Paris the accident occurred.

Police investigation has established that the Marquis' car was alone on the road at the time, and that it was without obstacles. All at once the car stopped short although the motor was still functioning perfectly and the tires were undamaged. There was a considerable shock and the car turned completely over, hurling the Marquis de Saint-Imier and the chauffeur out. The latter has a broken arm and possible internal injuries. The Marquis escaped with cuts and bruises.

From declarations made to the police the accident remains completely inexplicable. An examination of the car, which was badly damaged, showed that the motor, tires and other running parts were without defects.

Another auto passing the scene of the accident five minutes later, carried the chauffeur Pou-Hi to Estampes where he was placed in the hospital. The Marquis de Saint-Imier, after having received medical treatment, was able to take the Bordeaux express and continue his journey to Biarritz, where he is to be the guest of Señor Cuchillo, one of the most prominent members of the Argentine colony in France.

Gribal dashed into the laboratory, brandishing his newspaper.

"Did you see it, Professor? Decidedly, these scoundrels have all the luck."

Mazelier smiled.

"Never mind, Gribal, be calm. You forget that we also have had our bits of luck. Remember that Pou-Hi didn't succeed in running down Paulette either."

"Yes. But you saw that the Marquis alluded to some unknown force during the investigation. Don't you think that remark was addressed to us?"

"There is not the slightest doubt of it."

"And don't you think he will try an answer?"

"It is highly probable."

"And that doesn't stir you?"

"No use being emotional about it, my friend."

"Right. But that leaves us in the position of a condemned man waiting for the executioner. How are we going to defend ourselves?"

"Always in the same way that has been successful in the past."

And without giving Gribal time to answer, Mazelier went on:

"It mentions a Señor Cuchillo, Gribal. Do you know that *caballero* by any chance?"

"Cuchillo? *Parbleu!* He's a big race-track man and has a chateau in Corrèze. And I believe he is the author of what they call the Cuchillo syllogism."

"Ah, a syllogism. What is it?"

"Well, it was at a banquet last year that Señor Cuchillo said something like this—There are plenty of sheep in the Argentine. Now with sheep, one can make wool. With wool, one can make tapestries. Therefore we have a tapestry industry in the Argentine."

"Not a bad piece of reasoning if one admits that wool is all there is needed for tapestries."

His superior's calm and humor succeeded in reassuring Gribal.

"Well, Professor, what do we do next?"

The scientist replied: "Well, if you are willing, we will take a little trip. It will give us a change. Would you like to go with me?"

"Professor, you know very well, I would go with you to the end of the world."

"Take it easy, my friend, take it easy. The end of the world, that's quite a distance. And I can't leave for three days yet. So, in three days—"

"Yes," said Gribal, "a good deal can happen in three days."

"Things will happen, never doubt that. Then you will come?"

"And where will we be going?"

"To Biarritz," said Mazelier simply.

It is evident that if the Marquis de Saint-Imier had not lived in the center of society, the newspapers would have been silent about his auto accident. The celebrated "unknown force" which alone could have stopped Pou-Hi's car did not arouse much curiosity, for the very good reason that no one believed in its existence. Everyone who knew the Chinese—and these were a considerable number in the Passy section—had very clear opinions on the subject; Pou-Hi was a two-fisted drinker, and though he was also a splendid chauffeur, there was some talk. But Pou-Hi was one of those silent drinkers whose potations seem to make them more careful and more skillful.

When one intends driving from Paris to Biarritz in a single night, one has need of an extraordinary degree of strength.

Pou-Hi had strengthened himself by means of glasses of whiskey, taken in company with Suzie. Nobody doubted that the "unknown force" was a force from inside the bottle. Pou-Hi, sobered by the force of the accident, had simply told his master a likely story, and the latter had pretended to believe him.

Therefore, nobody in Paris thought of the Marquis any more, and Gribal was astonished to find the world very calm and very much inclined to mind its own business. The journey to Biarritz had to be held up; the scientist was having a series of interviews with the Minister of Science on the subject of the personnel of the office and its budget for the coming year.

But if Mazelier did not make his voyage, Madame Ghislaine Roberval took precisely the opposite decision at about the same time. Since the night when the fashionable world had seen her snub the Marquis at the ministry, she had decided to marry Monsieur Gabriel de Neuville, and she was distinctly worried. She knew the Marquis for a man capable of terrible revenges, and was certain that he would avenge the slight somehow. But when? And how? This rich and beautiful woman, who had everything needed to make her happy, could not avoid melancholy presentiments. It seemed to her that once she was married again, she would be in considerably less danger.

Her fiancé certainly made no objections. But Madame Roberval did not wish to be married in Paris. She feared some *contretemps* arranged by the Marquis, some noisy scandal that he might bring up.

"But what do you expect him to do?" inquired de Neuville. "I will notify the prefect of police, my dear Ghislaine, and I assure you that we will be thoroughly protected against anything of the kind."

Madame Roberval shook her head:

"No, Gabriel, no! We must not be married in Paris."

"But I must stay here for the present. I have been appointed secretary of this new international conference; the minister would never let me absent myself now."

"Try to accomplish the impossible, then. We must get away—to Italy or England."

"I would like nothing better. But I repeat, it is impossible. Besides, you know very well that the Marquis is at Biarritz now."

"Are you certain that it is not only done to deceive us?"

"Oh, certainly. He is there all right, and very busy. The fashionable world is talking of nothing but his eccentricities there."

Madame Roberval did not seem convinced. She did not know quite what she feared, and hardly wished to annoy her fiancé with nameless terrors.

What was she concealing? This: that in the voice of the loudspeaker in the Place de l'Opéra she also had recognized that of Saint-Imier! How could she confide to anyone, even her future husband, the terrors so vague that they seemed ill-founded which were stirring her? Neuville would certainly have laughed at her fright and remarked that the best loudspeakers deform the human voice to a greater or less extent. And after all, had the Marquis succeeded in his effort? No. Had he tried again?

No. The fact was that he seemed to have even abandoned his effort to pursue Madame Roberval.

These arguments, which her spouse-to-be would certainly have advanced, were a long way from convincing Ghislaine. She was quite certain that the Marquis had not in the least given up. And a strange thing had happened; she had seen him, in flesh and blood, following along the street, approaching as she went in the other direction, moving away when she approached, at the very moment when the society columns were publishing the news of her persecutor's being in another city and far away. The unhappy woman had arrived at the state of asking herself whether she were not the victim of hallucinations, but she confided her fears to no one.

Nevertheless, the day arrived when Gabriel de Neuville arrived with good news; the trip to Italy had become possible and with it a prolonged honeymoon. Madame Roberval found her lost tranquility in the announcement. She felt sure that as soon as she had become Madame de Neuville, she could arrange things so they would stay in Italy or somewhere else, anywhere else, provided it was not Paris.

Ghislaine was going to take the express to Vintimille. Her fiancé would follow by auto and meet her at Nice. Naturally Gabriel de Neuville accompanied her to the station and saw her safely installed in her compartment. They stayed, chatting for a few minutes while the train prepared for its departure. After about 20 minutes de Neuville glanced at his watch.

"The express is late already, my dear. If this keeps up I'll be in Nice before you are."

He laughed, not really annoyed at a delay which permitted him several moments more of conversation with her. But suddenly, glancing out of the window, he noticed a singular stir in the station. It looked as though all the travelers were getting out of the train. He got out with them. A hasty announcement was made:

"Breakdown somewhere. They're going to change locomotives. It will take at least 45 minutes. Take the express on the other track."

Neuville would have liked to ask more precise information, but the functionary who made the announcement had already disappeared, surrounded by a crowd of impatient passengers. The diplomat returned to Ghislaine and told her the news.

"Do you really believe that?" asked the young woman, incredulously.

"But... Anyhow, that's the official explanation."

"It won't hold water, my friend. You ought to know more than that about official reasons for things."

Madame Roberval spoke in a joking tone, but a strange feeling of disquietude rose in her.

"A breakdown before the engine has even started," she went on. "It's incredible. And that long to change locomotives. It's impossible. Well, let's change trains anyhow."

"I'll carry your bags. What a mob! It's odious."

The confusion was general, and everybody was talking at once. A voice arose, dominating the individual voices:

"The trains aren't running!"

Neuville, annoyed, grumbled:

"Ah, no, what are you telling us now? A joke, a little heavy, that joke. Why aren't the trains running? They arrived here, didn't they?"

As a matter of fact there were several trains stalled in the station.

But one had to admit it; none of them were moving.

CHAPTER XIII
THE VOICE AGAIN

Soon the news was coming in from every station of Paris, the inexplicable, phenomenal news. The fact, quickly verified, was that for some reason, not a train was running. The incoming trains rumbled in as usual; but they stayed.

The travelers, after having delivered the usual noisy protests which such a situation might be expected to call forth, went home. A good many of them, like Madame Roberval, did not give up their intention of traveling. If the trains were not moving, autos were. She, defying the conventions in this case of necessity, got into Neuville's car.

Neuville was delighted.

Unfortunately, when his comfortable car arrived near the city limits, he noted with annoyance that he was preceded by an interminable jam of vehicles of all kinds and descriptions, vibrating solemnly with the running of their motors, but utterly immobile. It was the world's record traffic jam.

Their horns made an infernal concert of noise. In the midst of it, Ghislaine and de Neuville noticed an employee of the *octroi* [4] running down the line, waving his arms and crying out something that nobody heard.

As he approached they heard him. "You can't get past!" he was shouting. "Autos and airplanes have been

---

[4] A tax collecting body. *Octroi* was a duty on various goods brought into certain towns and cities in France. It was abolished in 1948. (Ed.)

halted like the trains. Nobody has got out of the city for an hour."

This time Ghislaine was very frightened, and Gabriel was powerless to comfort her. What was happening was not the effect of chance; all the autos, all the vehicles of Paris, brought to a stop, but only when they tried to get out of the city.

Somebody was stopping them at his own good pleasure.

And who was this somebody if not the individual mad with hate who had already sown abroad so much terror?

"I tell you it must be him!" insisted Ghislaine.

"My dear," replied Gabriel, tenderly, "don't be frightened. One lone man would certainly not be able to do so much. This is probably due to some curious cosmic perturbation which we will read all about in tomorrow's newspapers."

Ghislaine shook her head but did not insist. All the same, the evident optimism of her fiancé reassured her a little, and she did not wish to destroy it. She kept her secrets to herself. But Gabriel secured her promise to see him in the morning, when they would go for a walk in the Bois and discuss the date of their marriage, which would take place in Paris since it could not be performed elsewhere.

But, that same evening in the capital where every inhabitant had found himself literally made a prisoner, and where the dumbfounded scientists were trying to explain the affair by means of scientific theories which they did not understand, the abhorred voice again took possession of the radio.

It was during a lecture given by Monsieur Reynier-Vitral on "the food of the future." The eminent chemist was developing the theme so often taken up and abandoned by successive generations of biologists that there is no such thing as life; the human animal being nothing but a machine, and that the best means of repairing the worn parts of this machine is not necessarily food as it is generally understood; that the stomach is not necessarily made to digest food, the teeth to bite it, or the palate to taste it; that everything can be expressed in the form of energy, and the energy the individual needs to recuperate himself can be furnished in the form of electrical currents of a certain character by special electrical machinery.

As the lecture was being delivered at the hour when most people had just finished well-rounded dinners, it amused them very much. Monsieur Reynier-Vitral spread his theories before a sympathetic audience, and if he had been able to hear the comments of his auditors, he would no doubt have been surprised to discover they were laughing at him.

Suddenly, at the moment when the speaker, lifting his voice, was about to introduce a touch of pathos, he was interrupted by a dry and somewhat insolent comment. The loudspeakers said:

"Enough! Monsieur Reynier-Vitral, shut up. You have said enough stupid things to last a year."

Immediately there was a reply. Monsieur Reynier-Vitral had evidently heard the remark, for he said:

"Oh, come, that's, not decent. Are you drunk, my friend?"

The lecturer must have thought that the voice came from the announcer just behind him.

"Monsieur Reynier-Vitral, don't insist! Your lecture is over. Nothing that you say will be heard. I am the only one who will be able to hear what you say. What? You

say you will complain to the authorities? Complain ahead, I wish you luck."

The public was amused, thinking it was something arranged in advance, like one of those scenes in the theater in which confederates in the audience answer the actors on the stage. That a person of the eminent respectability of Monsieur Reynier-Vitral should take such a part was a bit odd, but Paris contented itself with thinking that he must have been paid extremely well to take so ridiculous a part, a part which made all the other scientists of the world ridiculous at the same time.

A farce improvised by means of the radio, that was something really new! It was doubtless the first announcement of a great new discovery for once Reynier-Vitral had heard the other speaker, it was evident that it had become possible in some way for the hearers of a program to make the speaker hear them. What a vista! To be able to make the artist hear one's applause, hisses, or caustic comments, while one remained comfortably seated in one's armchair before the fire.

Or was it a joke on Reynier-Vitral? He would be the object of all the jesters of Paris the next day, and would probably sue the radio company for having asked him to lecture, and that would be the funniest of all.

Suddenly, amid the universal gaiety, the familiar voice fell like a douche of cold water.

"*Listen! It was I who threatened you all on the 18th of last October. You have already forgotten; you did not wish to understand. Remember the sudden dark, the terrible cold that you passed through. I wished to destroy the world, and you thought, I was crazy, didn't you? Because I did not complete the experiment, you said, 'It is impossible.'*"

In the different parts of Paris where loudspeakers were installed in public squares the crowd listened, curious but not scared. The unknown no longer frightened them; his bluff would end in a check, as before.

The voice went on: *"Haven't I given you sufficient proofs of my power?"*

In the Place de l'Opéra, a single voice rose:

"Razzberry!"

At the same moment, near the Etoile, another voice cried out:

"You'd think he was claiming he didn't do it."

The voice replied, with an indefinable accent of disdain:

"I didn't do it? You poor idiots; do you think I'm excusing myself, like a practical joker whose joke didn't come off? Listen! I am going to tell you my conditions; the conditions, Parisians, on which I will permit you to continue living."

The voice was silent for a moment, then went on with increasing violence: *"Listen! Listen! If you don't all want to be killed at the moment I have chosen, you must give up three victims to me. Two men and a woman. I wish the two men to perish like two animals, surrounded by the execration of their kind. Whoever tries to help them will perish with them."*

The actions of the crowd on hearing this singular explosion of anger resembled defiance more than fear.

Nevertheless, there were no voices raised in protest. The unknown, who struck from a distance, as though he were endowed with the gift of hearing and seeing everything on the spot, paralyzed the indignation of those who heard him because he remained hidden. Where could one find him, how could he be struck at?

A sort of savage laugh vibrated from the loudspeakers. Then the voice went on. *"I will give eight days to those I have mentioned to put an end to their existence. Let them be grateful to me for permitting them to choose their own forms of death, to commit suicide easily. If they have not died within the eight days there will not remain a single living being in the whole of Paris! All you who hear me now will die in the midst of the most frightful sufferings. But not all at the same time; for I have thought the matter over. Instead of killing humanity off at a single blow, I will slaughter it in detail."*

And the voice added, with another of its abominable laughs:

"It will be much more amusing that way. Now listen; this is my last public communication. I will not again warn you of my intentions. But you can expect some unpleasant surprises. Since last October I have perfected my apparatus. This time, nothing can halt me."

And suddenly, the voice became louder, more sonorous, to pronounce these terrible words: *"Have no pity on the men whose death I demand. They are nothing but highway robbers, assassins. I am going to give you their names, for they are cowards, they hide so that the people of Paris cannot find them to tear them in pieces. They are named—"*

The two names which should have been uttered were never pronounced! The loudspeakers carried to the crowd the noise of a brief clatter which was succeeded by silence, all the ordinary radio programs were off the air. Was it some new mystery? Then the voice came back, reinforced with new fury.

"Those who are trying to interrupt me would do better to be demanding my mercy. No one can leave Paris without my permission. I have today given you all

135

proof of that. What more do you need? Victims? You will not have long to wait. Beginning tomorrow I shall punish all those who are in my way. Listen! Listen! I am going to give you the names of the two men who shall die. They are—"

As on the first occasion, there was nothing but a confusion of burbling sounds. And then laughter—the laughter of the listeners was clearly audible. But the strange communication to the public was not ended.

"Listen, you who are laughing! You won't find it so funny tomorrow. For I now revoke the delay of eight days which you do not deserve. Tomorrow morning the first victims shall fall. I shall not stay my hand until you deliver the woman I hate over to me. The day after tomorrow she will be alone, in the middle of the Place de la Concorde. I shall go, I alone, to take her away from there, before all of you, who care to watch. For I do not fear you. You will see me tomorrow; I who challenge all of you will be there. And beware of trying to interrupt me; the man who attempts it will be struck by lightning. Do not try to deceive me; you will not succeed. The woman I demand, who is to be my slave is named—"

An agonizing silence. Then a voice, breaking on a note of rage and powerlessness:

"She is named—"

Another silence. A power as strong as that of the unknown was opposed to the appeal he was making to the fear and the egoism of the multitude. And rightly; if the three names were pronounced how many cowards in the crowds that heard the voice might not have hurried to carry out its bidding in the hope of saving their own lives?

But the names were never pronounced. The vast majority of those who heard were convinced they were listening to a supreme and unique exhibition of bluff. If the names were not given, it was because the man of hate at the other end of the broadcasting line had decided, at the last moment, not to give them.

People thought so. But the general curiosity was held at fever heat by the number of curious communications that came in during the night. In London, a voice, speaking the most perfect English, had declared through the loudspeakers there:

"From this time on, no French vessel will be able to reach any port in the British Isles. No airplane coming from France will be able to land on British soil."

The London public is less easy to stir than that of Paris. But the communication caused a lively emotion of surprise, for it was thought to be an official announcement. What did it mean? Was war against France to be declared?

A denial from the First Lord of the Admiralty and from the authorities in charge of aeronautics came a few minutes later to calm the aroused public. The denial was followed by the statement that the author of the false information was being searched for and would be punished.

But, on the following morning the news came in that the same announcement had been made over the radios of Brussels, Rome, Berlin, Moscow, Madrid, Lisbon, Athens and New York. When the differences in latitude and longitude were calculated it was discovered that all these broadcasts had followed each other within 15 minutes.

Eight more official denials followed each other in rapid succession.

What was it—a joker's syndicate abroad on the air? The same person, even granting the utmost speed of transmission, could certainly not have made himself heard in so many places at the same time. Evidently, the chief of this mysterious band must have assistants in all these cities.

But the international astonishment grew still greater when it was discovered that the different countries forbidden to French ships and planes, by the voice on the radio, received no more visitors from France. Some magical influence immobilized the great liners at a distance from the coasts. The airplanes were forced down before they had crossed the frontiers of France. And what was worse, it soon became evident that the international trains that left Paris were not arriving either. It touched various interests in their most sensitive spot; it upset the European equilibrium like a war. The situation was impossible.

But it had to be made possible all the same. Shipping companies, airplane companies, railroad companies, took the necessary steps to limit the disaster as much as possible. The halting of the international trains had brought with it the stoppage of the trains within the borders; long lines of immobilized railroad cars crowded the tracks. The ports along the Mediterranean and the Atlantic were less overcrowded, but they were rapidly becoming encumbered as the captains of ships hesitated to put to sea. At the airdromes, all was silence and stagnation.

A final surprise was yet to come for France; for all Europe. An attempt to organize traffic in trucks was begun; and every truck halted, out of order at the edge of the country.

This time doubt was no longer possible. The mysterious voices which had made their announcements in the cities of the world were not those of jokers. But they remained mysterious. And the opinion of Europe turned back to the threats made in the previous October and the phenomena that had followed them. What object had the man who was thus girdling France into immobility? And if he was, indeed, serious, who were the victims he had demanded?

It was noticed that the states of Central Europe had not received the mysterious communications, nor had any county outside Europe with the sole exception of America. All the scientists of the world turned their resources on the problem, to solve the questions it aroused, but above all to put an end to the blockade of France, for her isolation menaced all with some unknown disaster. And the scientists of the world remained in complete darkness.

But how had the communications been made? For it had to be admitted that France and all the other countries that had received the messages were covered with an enormous network of radiation.

CHAPTER XIV
THE FIRST VICTIM

At the National Office of Scientific Research there was feverish activity under Mazelier's direction. The Minister of Science had never hidden his view that this office should be a sort of discovery-factory. Consequently, it was Mazelier's duty to make discoveries.

Mazelier had smiled when this viewpoint was presented to him, and then said:

"Your Excellency may count upon me."

The "Excellency" discovered in this statement a sort of promise to get immediate results, and communicated the good news to the cabinet.

"You see! I called in Mazelier. I admit that I don't think a great deal of him. He is a little too sharp with that tongue of his. But I know men, and I touched this one on his weak point. I said to him, 'Mazelier, you must discover the means of restoring peace and security to the world.' And he answered, 'Excellency, I will do it at once.' Isn't that a bit of all right?"

Mazelier was even more on the right trail than the minister imagined. In the laboratory, for the tenth time, he was discussing a matter of tactics with Gribal.

"But I don't understand," said Gribal. "You only have to make a single motion to return things to normal. Why don't you do it?"

"Can't you imagine, my friend?"

"No. Time is passing. The delay which the Marquis has been so gracious as to grant us for our double suicide is already half over."

"Are you afraid, Gribal?"

"You know very well I'm not, Professor. Just the same, I admit that I would like to know how we're going to get out of this. The scoundrel has got himself a whole new set of teeth and claws."

"Let's look things over, Gribal. The Marquis wishes to get rid of us. Has he succeeded? He tried a vague allusion to us when he spoke of highway robbers. But he couldn't do more without revealing his own name. Before leaving for Biarritz, he tried to turn the minister against me, but he didn't push the point hard enough and the poor minister didn't understand. Finally, he wanted to give our names to the crowd, and I cut him off after having let him make his little speech. And since then, what has he done? He has made use of the same forms of radiation we used on him on the Estampes road. I admit that he has made progress. But he must be allowed to believe that we are still behind him. That illusion will help us a lot."

"And the woman he threatened at the same time as us?"

"Wait and see who she is, Gribal. As to seeing her alone in the Place de la Concorde, I would like it very much. Things wouldn't turn out the way the Marquis expects."

"But he will make victims."

"He says so. We shall see tomorrow. He can't do as much as he thinks."

"If we only knew where he is!"

"I would like to know that myself."

"Haven't you calculated?"

"Result, nothing. The only thing I can be sure of is that he has left Biarritz for Paris to try to stir up a mob against us. Since then I have lost track of him. And I admit that I cannot make out how he was able to speak in eight or nine places at once in so short a space of time. It's really quite wonderful."

"What he's doing now doesn't help you in locating him?"

"No. Perhaps he has an automatic apparatus. But anyway, there is no hurry, Gribal."

"What, no hurry? But we'll really have a catastrophe on our hands if this keeps up."

"Yes, but it won't keep up. We can end it whenever we wish. Only, the lesson must be rubbed in on the public. Do you remember the day after the catastrophe of last October? Nobody took the destroyer of the world seriously. Now he is stalling our economic life, and there is unanimous indignation. If I had intervened too soon, what would have happened? Do you see? Well, I will tell you if you don't—you and I, Gribal, would be finished. For nobody would have believed us when we came to reveal what we know."

"And now?"

"Ah, now it's a little different. Fear is decidedly the mother of wisdom. The minister sent for me a few minutes ago."

"And what did you say to him?"

"Naturally, that I was still in the dark."

"But…"

"But, Gribal, you forget that the Marquis de Saint-Imier is a personal friend of the Minister."

"Ah," cried the engineer, "really, you have a good deal of courage to continue the combat under such conditions."

"True," said Mazelier placidly, "the conditions are not too good. But I have a date tonight; in fact, I'm going there right away. Will you go with me?"

"Where is it?"

"To the Elysée."

"To the President of the Republic?"

"The same. It will not be the first time that the President has shared a state secret. Come along, Gribal, this time, they will believe us; there is a national danger."

The two men rose.

"The Devil!" said Gribal, "we're stepping out. To the Elysée Palace! But it's a little embarrassing; I am not used to places like that and I warn you that if it's going to be necessary to go through my paces before him, it might not turn out right. I think it would be a good job if I stayed here instead of going along to try out life among the flunkies."

Mazelier was ordinarily grave, silent and even a little reserved. But Gribal's fears sent him off in a burst of laughter.

"What an idea of etiquette in a republic you have! Haven't you had enough practice in the art of bowing? *Mon Dieu*, what will happen to us? I don't know any more about it than you do—they'll probably have us guillotined for kissing the floor at the wrong moment."

And the scientist added, with genuine sincerity:

"As a matter of fact, I probably know less about etiquette than you do."

And then, went on, with another laugh.

"We can practice a little before we start, if you like."

It was Gribal's turn to laugh.

"Bah," he said, "they will excuse us in view of what we have to say."

"Ah, this time you have touched the mark. And now, Gribal, listen—I have never met the President, but they tell me he's a good sort; just the kind of man we need, in fact. I don't think the etiquette question will worry him much."

Calmed by this soothing thought, Gribal started toward the door of the laboratory. He was about to open it when Mazelier cried:

"Stop! Don't open."

In the scientist's pocket his radiation-indicator was giving forth its characteristic buzz.

"You see, Gribal! The Marquis is not going to wait for the expiration of the 24 hours he gave us before we popped ourselves off. He's taking matters into his own hands. The good fellow actually thinks he can get us before we get to him."

"I ought to have thought of that," said the engineer. "Would you believe it?—I actually thought the Marquis would keep his word, and that we still had some time before us."

"Do you know what this rushing the program proves, though? That things are not going quite as well as our gentleman would wish. If he anticipates himself, it's because he's afraid of something. And that's queer, too, because except for shutting him up when he was about to give names, I have let him go ahead as he liked."

The revelator continued its buzzing.

"Hunt, go ahead and hunt for us," said Mazelier. We're safe here, old scout. My turn will come, too."

But Gribal could not repress a little shiver at the thought that a tiger's cage would have been a slightly safer place than the outer laboratory beyond the protection that Mazelier had thrown around their inner walls.

The indicator continued its annoying and hateful buzz.

"Decidedly, he must have determined to make an end of us today," remarked the engineer.

"Yes, but I have taken the necessary precautions."

And Mazelier continued with a statement that surprised his companion:

"If he can see and hear at a distance, he at least can't see and hear into this room."

To see and hear at a distance? Had the Marquis solved this problem also? And was Mazelier still undisturbed?

These questions hurried through Gribal's mind and he was the victim of a sort of discouragement. It was impossible to blink at the facts; Mazelier and he had before them an adversary as strong as themselves, provided with fully as much inventive genius and having the advantage of a lack of scruples that permitted him to do things they would not do.

Mazelier had understood from the start that they would have to use the same weapons as their antagonist. But that might injure innocent people at a distance— and all at once the engineer was terrified by the thought that the Marquis might be pursuing a parallel line of research. The man who had made his voice heard in all the great cities of Europe and America would certainly be able to distribute his malignant radiations abroad in several different places at the same time. And if one of these projections touched Gribal's house? He himself was safe—but his wife? and the children?

He could not remain still.

"Professor! I must try to get out!"

"You're crazy. Why?"

"Who knows what's happening at my home?"

Mazelier replied in a tone of authority:

"Nothing is happening there. Be calm. While he's busy here, he can't be thinking of other attacks."

"Are you certain?"

"Absolutely."

But Gribal's disturbance gave rise to several useful ideas for Mazelier. As a matter of fact the Marquis might very well be looking elsewhere than at the office for his enemies. Already, he had attacked the engineer at home, and had struck the exact spot. As a consequence, Gribal must not go home at all. And as a second consequence, his family must leave the Rue Boissy d'Anglas as soon as possible.

"You must move, my friend, to some distance from Paris, and without saying a word to anyone. Madame Gribal had better pack a few indispensables in a valise and clear out at once—but listen, tell her not to pack any trunks or make any ostensible preparations. Send all of them away this very evening."

"And how are we going to let them know? We are imprisoned here."

The rattle of the revelator continued.

"True," admitted Mazelier. "He's keeping us in here. I could get us out, but to do so would be to reveal to him that I know the forms of radiation that he is using, and that I have an answer to them, and he must be kept in ignorance of this. Patience, Gribal! He'll get tired of the game before we do, I repeat it."

Suddenly, the ringing of the revelator came to a stop.

"Quick! Let's go," cried Gribal.

"Wait a minute. No hurry."

Mazelier waited silently, his head on one side.

"Listen, Gribal. What did I tell you? It's starting again."

The buzzing started again; then halted, and went on in a series of fits and starts at irregular intervals.

"Good thing I'm on the job," said the scientist. "But something isn't going right with the Marquis."

There was a sort of pulsating of the buzzer and then as though the emission apparatus had reached the limit of its power, there was complete silence.

"This time I think we can risk it," said Mazelier. "Now, let's move fast when we do move."

Gribal, mad with impatience, threw open the door, and dashed down the corridor, followed by his superior. The two men arrived at the vestibule of the office. A tenth of a second and they were in the street; a half a minute and they were in the avenue. All at once, Gribal sank like an inert sack of corn to the pavement, and at the same moment the revelator vibrated for a second and then became mute once more. But Mazelier had the time to hear a sarcastic voice, which seemed to come from someone standing directly at his side, murmur:

"Got one!"

He looked around; he was altogether alone, with the inanimate Gribal at his feet.

Not altogether alone; for Roland Duplay was hurrying to help him.

The three Saint-Imiers were fighting among themselves with extraordinary violence. The Marquis was like a man fighting his own image in a mirror.

CHAPTER XV
THE HOUSE OF SILENCE

Paulette, like everyone else, had heard the new series of threats addressed to the people of Paris who had been guilty of incredulity in the face of the approaching destruction of the world. But this time, Roger's little jokes brought no smile to her lips. She understood the full significance of these threats, which left her mother so indifferent. After all, why should the good woman pay any attention to words which had no special significance for her?

And Paulette had been careful not to say: "But it is father and Professor Mazelier whose deaths are demanded." It would have uselessly frightened her mother and her brother. But the young girl's agony was all the greater because she had to conceal it.

And who could the woman be that the Marquis threatened at the same time? Paulette imagined that it might be herself. The Marquis must hate her because he had tried to assassinate her.

And thus, the girl had two good reasons for silence.

But, though waiting for her father's return, she refused to go to bed, overwhelmed with anxiety. It was even with some annoyance that she listened to the chatter of her brother, who rattled along:

"Isn't that amusing? There's a story for you. He's going to stop the trains, the airplanes and the ships. Pretty smart, that fellow. I'd like to know how he does it? I'll get it, though, and soon. I'm working on it like anything. I've been studying radiology, magnetism, chemistry, and electricity. I'll get beyond you one of these days. And then, you watch what I do!"

Roger was not really indulging in useless boasts. As he said, he was working hard and making genuine progress; and Paulette was watching him with not a little envy, for she was making no progress at all.

Since the afternoon, when Duplay had drawn her from the jaws of death, Paulette had not once seen him. The young man seemed bent on avoiding her. What a bashful youth! He was actually afraid to hear gratitude expressed in a harmonious voice accompanied with a charming smile and a glance from a pair of eyes filled with good wishes and sympathy.

To see him again would have been a real pleasure to Paulette. She searched for reasons to explain his over-discretion and finally found only one that satisfied her:

"He's afraid that I'll keep him from working," she told herself.

And then she scolded herself.

"But why should I worry about it. He's not accountable to me for his actions. I hope he's not sick, but if he isn't, then it's none of my affair."

She forced herself not to think about him, and thought she was succeeding. But Madame Gribal, worried at her uneasiness, kept asking her:

"Don't you think it's queer that your father hasn't come home yet?"

"No, mother. You know very well that father and Professor Mazelier were to work late tonight."

"Yes, that idiot on the loudspeaker again. But when your father has to work late, he always sends some message. And he hasn't sent any. *Mon Dieu*! I hope—"

"No, no, mother," Paulette hastened to say, though she herself was still more worried.

150

At midnight, Madame Gribal could no longer restrain herself.

"I'm going to the office," she declared. "You wait for me here."

Paulette replied:

"Mother, let Roger and me go with you."

"But if your father comes while we are out? He will be worried about all of us."

"I'll leave a note for him, on the table here. He can see it right away."

Paulette got a piece of paper and wrote on it: "Father, we have gone to the office to look for you. We'll be right back."

"There. He'll understand when he sees that. Are you coming, mother?"

The girl hurried into her wraps.

Roger asked: "Are you going to take a taxi?"

"Yes, yes," said the worried mother. "Come on, let's go. Hurry up, please!"

Three minutes later she was knocking at the door of Père Bibent's lodge.

"What are you doing here, Madame Gribal?" Her face showed so much worry and strain that he added: "What's the matter? Has something happened?"

"My husband has not come home. Is he still here?"

"I believe so... But certainly, Madame. I haven't seen either one of the gentlemen go out."

"Will you tell him I'm waiting for him here?"

"Right away, Madame Gribal. But you know, Professor Mazelier and he have stayed shut up in their laboratory all day long. I had some letters to take up, and when I knocked at the door no one answered. I think they didn't want to be disturbed."

Paulette was about to say: "You see, mother. They are busy."

But Madame Gribal, at the limit of her patience, would no longer listen to anything. She ordered: "Go on up. Knock until they open up. And if necessary, break in the door!"

Père Bibent was scandalized, but did not let it be seen. He went up the stairs as fast as his old legs would carry him. Five minutes went by—five centuries!

Père Bibent came back down. He was alone.

"I knocked and shouted," he explained, "but no one answered. I don't think there's anyone there."

Madame Gribal felt her knees giving way beneath her. Paulette had more courage; her father had repeated to her many times that she was never, under any circumstances, to lose her coolness of head. Neither fear, nor despair, nor pain, could prevent her brain from registering impressions, from reasoning, unless deprived of her senses.

"But you say that you haven't seen them go out!" cried the girl. "Then they must be in."

Afraid there would be a scandal, Père Bibent lost his head completely.

"But look," he babbled, "I haven't left my lodge."

"Think. You are certain? You haven't left your lodge for a moment, and you haven't seen anybody asking for Professor Mazelier or my father?"

"Oh, on that point, I'm certain, Mademoiselle. Nobody has asked for them."

"Then they must still be up there," repeated Paulette. "I'm going up to see for myself."

Père Bibent thought it over. All at once he struck his forehead with his hand, and said:

"But how stupid I have been! I was out three times during the day. Oh, not for a long time—a minute or two. Listen, Madame, the last time was not 20 minutes ago, possibly 15. Am I crazy or losing my memory? I went down to the corner of the Rue de Marignan for some tobacco. Just long enough to go there and back. Mademoiselle, it must have been then that they went out. Look, Madame, it could not be otherwise. For, as to being up there, they aren't. I made enough noise to wake the dead. They must be out."

Like a faithful echo Roger repeated: "Evidently. They must have gone out."

Paulette, somewhat more at ease, added: "See. Everything is explained now."

Père Bibent went on: "Madame, you must have missed your husband on the way. At the same moment you were coming to look for him, he went to find you."

"Let's go quickly, mother."

Thus brought back to hope, Madame Gribal permitted her children to lead her along. Moreover, the *concierge's* explanation was not impossible. And for that matter, in a few moments it would be decided.

As the taxi drew up at the door Paulette leaped out, leaving Roger the duty of accompanying their mother. She climbed rapidly up the stairs. Then she rang, hoping her father would open the door. But the door did not open. Paulette had to get out her key to get in.

In the entry she called: "Father! Here we are!"

No answer.

"Are you there, father?"

Paulette hurried through the dining room, her father's office, the bedroom, her own room and that of Roger.

Nobody! All the rooms were empty.

Madame Gribal and her son came in. When she looked at Paulette, it was unnecessary to ask a single question; she understood without words. Incapable of keeping up any longer, she gave one feeble cry and fainted.

Paulette perceived that it is sometimes difficult to keep one's head cool. A single sentence danced through her brain, "Father has not come home!" For a moment, she stood overwhelmed, inert, filled only with an immense distress. But the sight of her mother, flat on the floor before her, brought her back to her senses, and she bent to help her.

From her bedroom she brought the smelling salts, a carafe of water. What did one do? Paulette hesitated for a second, and then held the salts under her mother's nose.

After a moment she opened her eyes and began to move uneasily.

"Get some pillows!" called Paulette.

Roger hurried off to do it.

"Help me lift mother up. Good. Mother, mother! Are you comfortable now, mother? Do you hear me?"

Paulette, by a kind of instinct, knew that she must distract her mother's attention by an excess of words. But her mother had not quite come out of her faint; she was in a state of semi-consciousness in which she certainly did not understand the words her daughter was pronouncing so rapidly.

But Paulette, while continuing her chatter, found time to whisper over her shoulder to Roger: "Quick! Bring a doctor."

The boy did not even wait to put on a cap. He leaped for the door with the intention of racing down the four flights even more rapidly than he had descended them that morning, when he had slid down the banister.

But, having made a single bound, he came to a full stop before the door.

Paulette, surprised and angry, called to him: "Hurry up, you little fool! What are you waiting for?"

"Listen. Someone's coming up. They're right here."

"*Mon Dieu!*" cried Paulette. "Ringing our bell!"

Through her head flashed the thought:

If it were father he would come in without ringing?

She had not the strength to go to the door, but she braced herself for a shock. Only a bearer of ill news would call at so late an hour.

Roger had opened for the visitor. Paulette looked at her mother; Madame Gribal had heard the bell. She too, her hands joined and tense, awaited the blow of fate.

With a step that had an appearance of firmness she got to her feet and advanced toward the entry. Why didn't the visitor come in quicker? What was he saying to Roger? She wished to know, and at once.

At this moment, the visitor, accompanied by Roger, came into the dining room. Paulette gave an exclamation of surprise that was almost joyous. It was Roland Duplay!

"You!" she cried.

Then, suddenly, she was in confusion, hardly daring to lift her eyes. Roland placed a finger on his lips and held out a slip of paper, indicating that she was to read it before speaking.

Paulette read: *I have come on a mission for Monsieur Gribal. But, on your life, don't say a single word about it, aloud.*

Paulette passed the paper to her mother. The unhappy woman, at the end of her strength, lacked neither courage nor hope.

She glanced at the young man in a way that said more plainly than in words: "You have come from my husband. Is he dead or alive?"

Roland looked back at Madame Gribal and his severe face relaxed in a smile; the first Paulette had even seen on his face.

He took back the slip of paper and wrote upon it: "*Monsieur Gribal is now out of danger. He is waiting for you. I have a letter from him to give.*"

And Paulette wrote at the bottom of the paper:

"*Mother, Monsieur Duplay is all right. You can rely on him.*"

The young man pulled from his pocket an envelope, which he tendered to Madame Gribal at the same moment that Paulette passed her the paper, with the news concerning her husband.

Roger understood nothing of this singular scene. Why did everyone write notes instead of speaking? But as his mother and sister observed the same silence as their visitor, he imitated them.

Madame Gribal, meanwhile, was reading the letter from her husband:

My dear wife and beloved children:

I have just escaped from a terrible danger, but don't be worried, I am safe now. The danger threatens you, however, as long as you remain in the apartment. Fly, fly immediately. Don't wait to take a single thing with you. Follow the bearer of this letter; he will bring you to me. Don't speak to a living soul. I beg you, fly. In two hours we will be together again.

Gribal.

No doubt possible; it was the handwriting, the signature of the engineer. Nevertheless, Madame Gribal, happy though she was over the assurance of her husband's safety, was a trifle suspicious. Fly—but why? Immediately—but what about money? And where? And how would they go?

Ah, what a lot of questions remained undecided. But with Paulette it was otherwise. All worry disappeared, she felt almost joyous, as though she were already beyond all alarms and peril. What had already happened had been only the expected. As to what would happen in the future, she felt only that once the family was reunited they would be invincible. And moreover, Roland Duplay, once before her savior, was at hand.

She had become so habituated to the idea of miracles, among the extraordinary events through which they had been passing, that the appearance of the young man, at this time and place, seemed altogether natural. And as her father's wishes accorded exactly with her own, she had only to obey without discussion.

As soon as the fugitives had left the apartment, Paulette closed the door noiselessly. The concierge let them out without being spoken to, and there remained only the people who lived on the floor below, who must have thought they were going to the theater rather late in the evening.

In the Rue Boissy d'Anglas, Duplay silently motioned for them to follow him. He led the way up the street, almost to the Madeleine, turned into a covered passage at the left, and came out on the Rue Faubourg Saint-Honoré. There, a powerful car was drawn up at the curb. The young man opened the door.

"Get in, mother," whispered Paulette.

Madame Gribal thought she must be dreaming. To bolster up her courage she repeated to herself the words her husband had written: "In two hours we will be together again." Two hours in an auto—at least 75 miles. She got in. Roger and Paulette took their places beside her. The girl left the door open, thinking that Duplay would join them.

"But where is the chauffeur?" asked Roger, forgetting the injunction to silence.

Madame Gribal understood no better than her son what danger there could be in speaking aloud a few feet from the Rue Royale. Roger's question seemed to have something in it; she glanced at Paulette.

She, who looked at the door with something like regret, silently indicated Duplay, who had installed himself at the wheel.

The sight left her a little thoughtful, for Roland could hardly have a very clear notion of the right way of piloting a 100 HP car.

Nevertheless, everything went well. Duplay apparently knew the geography of Paris to perfection, for with singular accuracy, he followed all the least frequented streets, and those where there were the fewest encumbrances. He conducted them thus to the Place des Ternes, turned to the right, ran along the length of the exterior boulevards and arrived at the Porte de la Chapelle.

By this time Paulette was certain that the wheel was in experienced hands.

But he stopped 100 yards from the *octroi*. What was there to stop them? Roger, with his cap pulled down over his eyes, stuck his head out for a peek.

"Traffic jam," he whispered.

Fifty or more vehicles, with more coming up every moment, waited, silently. Paulette understood. Roland had run into that unknown force which was blockading all the Parisians in Paris.

But, what now? For Paulette recognized that this second blockade could very well have been established to keep the car, for which Gribal was waiting somewhere, in Paris. She understood that the injunction to silence had not been imposed upon them without some reason. And Roger had twice broken it, and her mother, who sighed out her impatience and renewed fear in a series of gasps.

She glanced at Duplay. He turned at the same moment, met her eyes, and gave her a nod which signified: "Don't worry."

Then, while the rest of the lineup made a terrific hubbub with their horns and voices, he descended from the driver's seat to draw down all the curtains that seemed to be made of leather, and were placed outside the car.

In the interior the darkness was complete. Madame Gribal was the prey of terrors. She would not have hesitated to leap from the car and return to the Rue Boissy d'Anglas had she not held her husband's letter firmly clutched in her hand. As to Roger, he would certainly have made a racket if his sister had not suddenly placed her hand over his mouth.

But neither the fright of the mother nor the annoyance of the son were of long duration. The interior of the auto was lit with a strange and feeble luminescence, sufficient for the occupants, but not enough to pierce the outside curtains. At the same moment there came a terrific racket outside, the sound of many voices.

"At last! Not too soon, I'll say."

"Let's go."

"It was a joke."

"Farewell, dear heart. I'm off to the country."

"Hey, everybody! Good-bye and thanks."

Shouts of all kinds came from the chauffeurs of the vehicles in the line ahead of that which held the Gribal family. They felt the car slowly getting into motion, following the others which were crossing the barrier.

But to their profound surprise, it seemed to Roger and Paulette that cries of rage and imprecations were coming from the drivers of the cars behind them, and then from the drivers of those which were all about.

Had they not moved after all? It sounded as though a hole in the invisible curtain had opened before Roland to shut down again immediately behind him.

But the auto began to travel with a velocity that gave Madame Gribal the sensation that they had left the earth and were flying. Then they gradually slowed down; the pale light went out suddenly, the auto stopped; the leather curtains went up again, and a voice pronounced the following delightful words in the midst of the peaceful night:

"Madame, we are safe, and we will arrive in ten minutes. You can speak as loud as you wish now."

Roger profited by the permission to say: "Don't let anything keep you from going as fast as you like. Speed is very agreeable to me."

CHAPTER XVI
AN AUDIENCE WITH THE PRESIDENT

Ghislaine Roberval had guessed better than Paulette at the name of the woman the Marquis had wished to announce to the mob. Why had Saint-Imier not given it after the preliminaries? The idea that a power as strong as his own had prevented him did not occur to her.

She had promised her fiancé to meet him in the Bois de Boulogne. Dare she keep the appointment? Not to go would be to worry Gabriel de Neuville, who, like everyone else, had heard the Marquis' threats, and already knew enough to be able to guess the rest. But to go—would that not be to place herself in the lion's jaws?

But after all, what would she be risking? She would go—and immediately. Nevertheless—fear paralyzed her. If the Marquis should have accomplices? If one of them had been told to kidnap Ghislaine Roberval? A kidnapping in broad daylight—Saint-Imier was quite capable of so audacious an action.

Ah, how she regretted the past, when still a young girl she had been flattered to see the Marquis paying attentions to her. She had imprudently accepted his advances until the day when chance had allowed her to see his basic character, vile and cruel. She was certain, now, that the Marquis would stop at nothing... Well, in that case, the thing to do was to be with her fiancé, who would be able to defend her.

She went to the Bois. Gabriel was already waiting near the Pré Catalan. As usual, he was calm and smiling, and seemed unconscious of any possible danger.

"My dear Ghislaine, I hope that the ridiculous announcements that everybody has been hearing, have not disturbed your sleep?"

"Alas, yes! I'm really frightfully worried."

Neuville began to laugh: "Why? Because a practical joker wants to gather a big crowd around the Place de la Concorde this afternoon?"

"You're laughing? But why has the crowd been invited? Can't you imagine what woman he was talking about?"

"My dear, keep cool, and don't worry. Of two possibilities, one must be a fact, either it's the Marquis de Saint-Imier with one of his excesses again—and if it is, I promise you that I, for one, won't hesitate to denounce him. He's beginning to be annoying, that animal. Now, if it isn't he—"

"But it is, Gabriel, I don't doubt it for a minute."

"In that case, he can come to the Place de la Concorde as he has announced. He will find me there to pull his nose for him."

"Gabriel, don't go."

"I beg your pardon. I shall be the first one on the spot."

"But this man has extraordinary methods of…"

"*Parbleu!* Do you think so?"

"But this blockade of Paris and then of all France?"

"My dear Ghislaine, according to what I heard at the Ministry of Foreign Affairs, the Marquis had nothing to do with that. Do you know what caused it? A Japanese scientist living in Russia has made an enormous electromagnet with extraordinary powers, and he is performing some experiments at our expense, that's all."

"But the Marquis is using the results of those experiments. He has said as much."

"Bah! He's a boaster. It's another of his lies."

Ghislaine and Gabriel were alone, all alone, in a little glade. All at once they heard a voice near them murmur:

"*Diplomats who talk too much never get anywhere.*"

Gabriel cried: "Who is following us?"

He looked around, but saw nobody.

Madame Roberval, trembling, had let go his arm. She was about to say: "It's the Marquis' voice."

But she did not have time. Gabriel de Neuville, as though struck by lightning, rolled at her feet.

"*Got two!*" cried a strident voice.

Ghislaine would have cried out, screamed for help, but she remained mute with terror; the Marquis, grinning terribly, stood suddenly before her. It was like an apparition; for he vanished as he had come...

A suddenly-organized search failed to find any trace of anyone. The examination of Gabriel de Neuville's body failed to show the slightest trace of a wound. It was thus established that what Ghislaine declared to be a crime was nothing but a sudden heart-failure on the part of her fiancé.

Mazelier did not care much for official society, and the President of the Republic was reported to be not particularly fond of that of scientists. But Mazelier had to lay before the head of the country, who understood nothing of such subjects, the reasons why France was cut off from the rest of the world and Paris from the rest of France. How would he manage to do it?

On his side, the President expected to see before him a man filled with the pride of recondite information who would tell him a great many incomprehensible

163

things and make a lot of demands he did not wish to meet. It was impossible to believe that the man who, they told him, was the only one in France capable of saving the situation, would not ask for very considerable rewards.

Mazelier and the first magistrate of the Republic were, therefore, equally on their guard when they found themselves in each other's presence in the presidential office. They looked at each other…and suddenly their strained faces relaxed a little. They had, by a species of telepathy, seen themselves in each other, equally simple, equally enemies of bunk and useless words. The ice was broken immediately.

"Professor Mazelier," said the President, "I beg you to be seated."

"Thank you, Monsieur le President. I have not yet slept tonight and—"

"You have been working continuously, and I have doubtless interrupted you in sending for you. But you understand the situation. This blockade, to which we are submitted, is both ridiculous and terrible. Can you get us out of it?"

"Very easily."

"And when?"

"Right away, if you insist. I may add that if I have not already ended it, it is for excellent reasons, which I ask your permission to lay before you."

"Speak! Speak!" cried the stupefied President.

"I have voluntarily allowed this state of affairs to continue, although it is truly embarrassing, in the hope that the man who brought it about will be obliged to come out in the open."

"But we know who it is!"

"Really, Monsieur le President?"

"The information is certain. It is a Japanese scientist, with a new electromagnet, who has caused it."

A burst of laughter, in defiance of etiquette, shook the presidential assurance a trifle.

"You don't agree with that, Professor Mazelier?"

"Not for a minute, Monsieur le President. The author of the blockade of Paris is in possession of formidable weapons. He is threatening the most abominable crimes and he has already committed some this night."

"What?"

"Yes; it is the same man who dared to invite the public to a new type of spectacle at the Place de la Concorde."

The President remained incredulous:

"I believe," he said, "that you are confounding two things; a joke and a scientific experiment. Both of them are guilty of upsetting the—"

"Both are criminal, Monsieur le President."

"In any event, it is hardly permissible to play a public joke of that character. Well, Professor Mazelier, since you can open the frontiers of Paris and of the country, I ask in the name of the country that you do it without delay."

It was an order. Mazelier bowed: "I cannot obey you as yet," he declared clearly.

"Because you are unable?"

"I left Paris tonight, Monsieur le President. I had to take to a place of safety, outside the city, because my collaborator, Gribal, was struck down under my very eyes, by the murderous radiation with which the criminal is menacing the entire population."

"And you said nothing to the police?"

Mazelier risked a slight shrug of his shoulders:

"The Prefect of Police can do nothing against a man whose very name is unknown to him, and which he will be unable to discover unless I tell it."

"You know, then—this individual?"

"Yes, Monsieur le President."

"And you will not give the name to the officers of justice?"

"No; for it would be to make certain of failure."

"But will you tell it to me?"

"I came here to tell you everything. The man, whose science and audacity make him so dangerous and so capable of escaping justice and who has not been touched because of his position, is the Marquis de Saint-Imier."

The name made the President start. "Saint-Imier! Impossible! But you are—"

The President stopped himself, just in time, from saying "You are crazy." He went on: "You are certainly mistaken. Saint-Imier! Everyone in the cabinet knows him. He has a colossal fortune."

"Yes, Monsieur le President. That is all true, and more. But in running down the person responsible by means of my scientific apparatus, I found the Marquis de Saint-Imier. That is the plain, brutal fact."

"But, if your apparatus made a mistake?"

"Impossible. Besides, I have checked it in a dozen ways. I am certain of what I am saying."

"Your name and your attainments inspire the utmost confidence, but I must tell you that I don't believe you."

"Time will tell, Monsieur le President."

"Time! Time! But time has been running on without bringing any information but the unlikely hypothesis you have just advanced. This is hardly very good. You can liberate the stalled traffic of Paris and of all France and you refuse to do it because you have a theory about who is causing the trouble."

"If you were persuaded that I were telling the truth, would you blame me, Monsieur le President?"

The question touched the heart of the matter. The President, who was becoming angry, became calm again.

"Perhaps," he conceded. "Unfortunately, I am not persuaded. Saint-Imier! But it's absurd. And you—"

The ringing of the telephone interrupted the conversation and the President must have found the information it gave him interesting, for with a gesture, he invited Mazelier to take an extension. The scientist heard:

"...there are more than 50,000 persons gathered around the Place de la Concorde to see the arrival of the man of the radio. It is now 2:45 p.m., and nobody has come, naturally. People are already beginning to leave. Order is perfect and the crowd is calm."

"Come," said the President, "admit that you were wrong to take a bad joke so seriously. Believe me; relieve the blockade if you can, and think no more of the poor Marquis who doubtless does not even know you are talking about him."

The audience was over, and Mazelier was left in confusion. The scientist was about to rise and take his leave, when a sharp voice resounded through the room from the loudspeaker which the President, like the meanest citizen of France, kept in a corner. And the voice in mocking accents, was making a new series of threats:

"Parisians, you are laughing because I didn't keep the appointment I made for this afternoon. Wait for a few minutes and you will laugh no longer. I have already accomplished a portion of my vengeance; the woman

who should have been given to me is mourning her dead fiancé now. Let her take her lesson from this. And I have already demanded once, that you sacrifice the two men I hate. Professor Mazelier and Gribal! Mark those names. Gribal was already struck down last night; now let Mazelier tremble. He will not escape me, even behind the barred doors of his office. And his death will be frightful!"

Silence. The President of the Republic gazed dumbfounded at Mazelier. The scientist, in spite of the injunction, was not trembling.

Sharply the voice went on: *"Parisians, you will now feel the weight of my anger. I could kill you by the hundreds; but I prefer to kill you one by one. I will exterminate you in detail; it will be more amusing."*

A laugh at this lugubrious joke came from the mouth of the loudspeaker. And the voice continued:

"In an hour you will have 20 victims to prove that I can do what I say, and that I meant what I said when I demanded the sacrifice of the three persons as the price of your lives. And that is not all; ten children will fall dead. Every day, do you hear, every day, there will be ten more deaths, chosen by chance in the city. Nothing can prevent them; useless to try."

Mazelier was by now as overwhelmed as he had been calm before.

"There is not a minute to lose!" he cried. "Monsieur le President, give me permission to act."

A suspicion crossed the mind of the head of the state. He wondered whether Mazelier himself had not organized this affair with the aid of some accomplice. But the absurdity of such a suspicion was all too evident. And then?

Mazelier was on his way to the door when a servant appeared.

"Monsieur le President, a lady in mourning insists on your receiving her at once. It is Madame Ghislaine de Roberval."

This name, though unknown to Mazelier, was not unfamiliar to the President. What could the most beautiful and fashionable woman in Paris be wanting?

"In mourning?" inquired the President. "I thought she was about to be married."

He gave the order that she should be admitted. It was a day of surprises, and the normal order of etiquette must give way before the necessities of the situation.

Ghislaine entered, pale as a ghost.

"What can I do for you, Madame?"

"Monsieur le President," she said in a voice broken with tears, "I ask for justice. Justice against the cowardly assassin of Gabriel de Neuville."

"What? Monsieur de Neuville…"

"…Was struck down this morning at my side while we were walking in the Bois de Boulogne. It was a crime. And I swear that the author of the crime was the Marquis de Saint-Imier!"

The President turned: "Go, Monsieur," he said to the scientist. "I believe you and I place the resources of the state at your disposal."

"Alas!" said Mazelier, "this time I am arriving too late."

CHAPTER XVII
UNMASKED

Mazelier was fully aware that he would not have received the presidential carte-blanche without Ghislaine's sudden and dramatic interruption. He had stirred, but not convinced his auditor. Doubtless the President had been ready to admit that the director of the Office of Scientific Research was beyond suspicion, but so was Saint-Imier. How could he suspect the personal friend of half the cabinet, the man whose money, liberally disposed, had done so much for science and education? Mazelier had seen for himself that the head of the state did not take the radio threat seriously. Alas, these threats were only too serious. The Marquis had announced that the first deaths would occur within an hour. In ten minutes Mazelier would be in his laboratory ready for the struggle. He would begin by lifting the blockade as he had promised the President. And then he would undertake the counter-offensive against Saint-Imier. But where was he? In the Rue Cortambert? It was unlikely. And Mazelier asked himself:

"For that matter, will I reach my laboratory alive? The brigand can see and hear at a distance, and he must be watching me. By going to the office, won't I fall directly into the trap? He thinks Gribal is dead, but he knows I'm still in the ring. Should I expose myself? Well, so much the worse, my duty is clear. Roland is waiting for me at the office."

And as he hastened along, Mazelier-continued to himself:

"He's right, that Marquis. I should not leave my laboratory. He has made use of the time while I was away at the Elysée, and he has been able to give my name and Gribal's to the mob. Well, we will see. At any event, he has not divulged the name of the woman he pursues so furiously. That name—I know it now, it is Ghislaine Roberval. Well, well, Marquis, we'll see."

Mazelier, having just arrived in the Champs-Elysée, was about to go up to the Rue de la Boëtie, when he encountered a veritable tide of humanity. A shouting crowd was pushing in the direction of the Etoile, crying: "Assassin! Death to the assassin. Down with the baby-killer!"

It was the sound of a revolution in birth. But what revolution, and against whom?

This is what had happened: the crowd of the curious assembled around the Place de la Concorde, at the moment when Mazelier was having his conference with the President, amused themselves with their own remarks at first. Everybody was perfectly sure that nothing at all would happen. The public mind had been made up; the experiments of the person they had come to consider as a kind of scientific acrobat, juggling with radiation as an athlete with dumb-bells, were doubtless very curious, but were always a little behind the program he laid out for himself.

Briefly, he was bluffing. The end of the world had been promised; the transport of France had been disorganized, and for what? Nothing at all, when you came down to it. The Earth continued its march through space; the Sun rose every morning, and people went about their business. The unknown made continual threats and then did little or nothing. But what he had said this time had a personal interest for the whole population.

171

"It's him again? Bah, I'm too much in a hurry to listen. Tell me about it next week," said a man who was taking a bus in the Rue Chateaudun.

"Yes, yes, but listen. It's really amusing this time. Listen," called someone from a table on the corner, where he was seated before a glass of vermouth-cassis.

A circle of auditors gathered around the loudspeaker whose voice dominated the noise of the vehicles in the busy street.

When the voice pronounced the names of Mazelier and Gribal, they produced a veritable torrent of jokes. The two scientists became famous in a second; and they attained the notoriety to which their genuine discoveries entitled them without having to work for it.

"The guy's a nut," cried one gentleman comfortably seated at his café table. "Bright idea, to use the radio to announce that he's having a quarrel with Mazelier and Gribal!"

This was the common opinion. But a wave of uneasiness went over the crowd when the voice raged on to announce the deaths of ten persons taken by chance. It was a little beyond the license permitted to jokers. Nevertheless, the threat would not be carried out. At this moment Mazelier and Gribal would have received a public ovation if they had appeared. As the oration from the radio ended, there were murmurs of disapproval:

"It's time somebody squelched that idiot!"

And there was a general shrugging of shoulders. There are certain crimes impossible to commit, especially when one announces to the public that they are about to be committed. Nobody doubted that the prefecture of police had been warned and detectives were already on the job. And the individual who had already been looked for could expect a rough handling when they found him.

It would not be too hard—broadcasting stations are not difficult to locate.

As a matter of fact the prefecture and the police were working. The news that they were searching for the origin of the voice, followed the voice itself without a moment's delay and had the effect of calming the mind of the public still more.

All at once there came a piece of news that was like a clap of thunder. While people were listening in the center of Paris a terrible drama had been taking place in the outskirts. Ten children in Passy had been stricken, covered with terrible burns. The crime had been committed, and the assassin had not even had that kind of cynicism which permits a criminal to keep his word exactly; after having sought the aid of the Parisians, he had deceived them. As cowardly as he was cruel, he threatened at one place and struck at another.

But could one believe what was said; the horrible details that were passing from one quarter of the city to another by word of mouth? Alas, to those who would have liked to have doubted the crime and its terror there came confirmation from the criminal himself as the loudspeakers once more resounded with the well-recognized voice:

"*Parisians, do you believe me now?*"

The assassin was triumphant and his laughter an insult. He went on: "*I have kept my promise. Justice is done on the wicked city!*"

There was in the crowd a ground-murmur that contained at once the seeds of fury and revolt.

The scoundrel dared to speak of justice! He went on: "*For today, that is all. You are at liberty. All of you can go about your business. But I warn you that if Mazelier is still alive by tomorrow, 20 children will pay the*

173

forfeit for him; on the following day 40, and the day af-
ter that 80, and so on. Until the day when you have ob-
eyed me and given him up to justice! I want that man!
Good night, Parisians; I have no more to say to you but
that nothing will stop me now."

Fists were clenched toward the loudspeakers as
though the inanimate machines could have transmitted to
the unknown these evidences of the general anger.

And it was almost as though they had, for the voice
took up again: *"You didn't take me seriously, did you?*
Don't complain now, I gave you plenty of warning. But
be warned; if you do not obey me, I will kill every child
in Paris, and then the rest of you, one by one. I hate you,
citizens of Paris; everything you suffer only increases my
pleasure. Your anger, your fears are delicious. I hate
you, all of you!"

The entire city was literally in the street, moving
aimlessly about, and resembling one of those prodigious
tidal waves which carries everything before it. The formidable murmur of revolution mounted; a breath, a
sound, would turn it in one direction or another. There
was not one person in a 100,000 of those who heard who
had ever seen or heard of Mazelier and Gribal, but the
two names, let loose in a dozen streets by voices raised
in genuine anger, became the symbols of the resistance
and defiance the crowd offered to the unknown menace.

"Vive Mazelier! Vive Gribal!" shouted thousands
of voices in different parts of the city.

A final mockery came through the loudspeakers:

"Yes, Vive Mazelier! But add Death to Paris! after-
ward."

The voice said something more but nobody heard or
wished to hear; the mob was up; the church bells that
had sounded for the deaths of kings, tolled in Paris, and

the sections were choosing delegates to call on the President. There, they were received with courtesy and given the latest details in possession of the authorities.

Ten children had been attacked by the mysterious forms of radiation at regular intervals of three minutes. A half an hour had been enough for the multiple assassination. But, among these ten children, one had miraculously escaped the agony of the others. The escaped child lived in the Rue Duphot; attacked at exactly 3:45 p.m., he had suffered agonies for a few minutes, and then his tortures had ceased and his burns had quickly disappeared.

The other nine had succumbed under conditions which left the witnesses altogether incapable of describing the event. What kind of radiation had been used? How was it that the first child attacked had escaped the danger? These questions would be studied later; for the moment, the entire population had a double duty; first to prevent more crimes and second to discover the criminal.

Now, at the Elysée, chance or providence had ruled it so that the servant who had introduced Madame Roberval had waited in the outer office. He had good ears, and the name of Saint-Imier, pronounced with such energy by Ghislaine, repeated with stupefaction by the President and with an accent of triumph by Mazelier, had reached his ears. And when the delegations from the sections arrived he could not restrain himself from affirming:

"It's the Marquis de Saint-Imier!"

Nobody thought of doubting, such is the unreasoning passion of a French mob, once aroused. From the courts of the Elysée to the Faubourg Saint-Honoré, from the Faubourg to the Champs-Elysée and the Place de la Concorde, the news ran like a fire through a train of powder, and a few minutes later, as the cabinet was in session, it was hurled even there into the midst of the discussion. The Minister of Science, vibrating with indignation, cried:

"I protest against the calumnies which are being spread abroad! An occasion for public mourning should not serve as the pretext for absurd accusations."

But it was noticeable that the President of the Republic did not support the protests of his minister. Nevertheless, the latter went on:

"Come, come. It's foolish to raise such accusations against a man of the importance of Saint-Imier without cause and without proof. I dined with him only yesterday evening."

The Minister of the Interior answered:

"Ah, my dear fellow, if every other murderer only knew that a sure means of avoiding suspicion was to invite you to dinner!"

Everyone recognized that because a man was rich was no reason for exempting him from justice. But what could be done without proof? And there was no proof.

It was the President of the Republic who cut the knot of the difficulty:

"There is no reason," he declared, "why we should not make an investigation. In a moment as grave as this, I need not add, I suppose, that we should take precautions that the inquiry should not be influenced from any quarter whatsoever. Justice must be done without weakness. But on the other hand, such an inquiry will keep the people of Paris from being carried away by momentary impulses."

It was impossible to object to these words of wisdom. The Minister of Science no longer opposed, and his colleague of the department of Justice went into immediate conference with the heads of the prefecture of police.

Meanwhile, the President had another subject of worry. What had become of Mazelier? The scientist, when he asked for complete liberty of action, had doubtless intended to signify that he would pass into a prolonged eclipse from the public gaze. But only one of two things was possible; either the scientist knew nothing of the Marquis' latest crime, and therefore, since he was ignorant, was inferior to him, or, Mazelier knew about it and his efforts to prevent the crime had been futile. For if Mazelier were aware of what was going on, it was impossible to suppose he would not have done everything to prevent the crime.

Also, the head of the state wondered whether the child who had been saved had not owed his life to Mazelier. But why had only one escaped? In any case, bound by the promise he had given to Mazelier, the President could not confide his impressions to anyone.

Meanwhile, events were driving on in a manner altogether unforeseen.

While the official powers were discussing the method of an inquiry, which was considered a matter of extreme delicacy, difficult and extremely confidential, the people, stirred by the obscure atavism of self-defense, were on their way to perform the same task without official permission.

From all directions, without an order being given, the people were gathering. Let the assassin defend himself by the emission of his murderous radiation. The people would see whether he was capable of striking down an entire population. The radiations tamed by the Marquis made him redoubtable, no doubt, but could his powers really extend to infinity?

Every street of Paris became filled with a human river, all flowing in the direction of the Rue Cortambert and the home of the Marquis. The crowd was all the more formidable because it remained silent. Not a cry, not an imprecation, not a gesture. But silently, it moved along, every member animated by the same thoughts like different drops of water in a tidal wave.

In a few minutes the Rue Cortambert was filled by that flood, which halted before the great mansion of Saint-Imier, with its double doors, the back-eddies piling up in all the adjoining streets.

With the irresistible force of a tide the mob went through the doors, and then, despite the protests of the doorman, into the grand hall of the building itself.

Then, and only then, was the invasion provided with some sort of organization.

Two companies were formed to explore the different parts of the building. One remained in the entry hall to question the domestics and centralize whatever information was obtained. A footman, with a suspicious eye and proud lips, tried to halt the invaders at the foot of the grand stairway. He was seized by iron hands. Frightened, he babbled:

"What do you want here?"

"We wish to see your master!" said a rude voice.

"But Monsieur the Marquis has gone out."

"We will wait. Get your comrades, the other servants, together, and bring them here."

Between two bodyguards the footman led the way toward the office, while the searchers began to explore the four floors, the cellars and the vast garages of the Marquis.

What would they find?

CHAPTER XVIII
THE SECRET OF THE STAIRWAY

It must be remembered that the different incidents of this inquest all took place together, although they are narrated here in sequence; and the intervals between them are intervals of a few seconds only. It was swiftly established:

1. That the servants of the household were all there, with the exception of a housekeeper called Suzie la Bretonne and the chauffeur of the Marquis, the Chinese, Pou-Hi. Where were they? The others could give no information on this point.

2. All the servants were agreed in stating that the Marquis de Saint-Imier had gone out, alone, about 20 minutes before, in the little town car he kept for running errands around Paris. The fact that he had taken this car indicated to the others that he intended to return early.

Nothing abnormal about any of this. But suddenly they were in the midst of impossibilities.

The servants, after having said there were but three loudspeakers in the mansion, one in the little salon on the ground floor, the second in the Marquis' room and the third in the rooms reserved for the use of the help, added that they had as usual turned it on during their lunch. That a little later, their loudspeaker, as well as that in the little salon, had suddenly ceased functioning in the midst of the concert, and that afterward, having heard nothing else, they imagined something had gone wrong with the apparatus. Questioned as to the threats which had come over the air subsequently, and had been heard from every radio in Paris, they affirmed, with the utmost apparent sincerity, that they had heard nothing at all.

Thus there were two possibilities:

Either the servants were all in agreement to tell the same lie, and in that case, it would be necessary to assume that the Marquis had extended his circle of accomplices to a dangerous size,—for when there are so many, the result is that one of them always tells.

Or, they were telling the truth, and the disconcerting fact must be admitted that, alone in all Paris, the loudspeakers in the Marquis' mansion had remained silent at the precise moment when the assassin was boasting of his crimes.

If this fact was not directly incriminatory it was at least indicative. It could mean that the Marquis de Saint-Imier had found a means of speaking to the rest of the world without being heard in his own household.

A second report, from the group which was searching the rooms on the second floor, added to the uneasiness which everyone felt in this luxurious house. The Marquis' bedroom was on this second floor, reached through an ante-chamber next to a bathroom. There was a striking contrast; all the furniture of the ground floor, including the dining rooms, was of an extraordinary richness, almost too rich and elegant; all the furniture of the second floor was made up of pieces of surprising elegance, veritable museum pieces.

But the ground floor furniture was garish and absurd, that on the second floor, refined and in the best of taste. Second contrast; the windows on the ground floor contained jewels, set in the worst possible style; but, on the second floor, the windows were stained glass in indisputable taste. The same thing was true of the pictures which covered the walls, but in a different way.

The ground floor was filled with the latest works of the moderns, hideous and popular. But the enormous bedroom contained only a single canvas, a wholly admirable portrait of a woman. In a corner of this portrait a card had been placed. It bore the name of Saint-Imier and these curious words:

I loved her. Now I hate her.

No one in the mob could recognize the portrait as one of Ghislaine Roberval.

But the visitors were not in the Marquis' private residence to look over his art treasures and furniture; they were there to find proof that an atrocious crime had been committed in the house. There ought to be a wireless station in the building. But no such place had been found, though it would be in the upper floors near the bedroom, in the most reserved part of the house.

The search party was about to go back over its tracks, when one of its members, an interior decorator, whose models of new designs for furniture bore witness to a remarkable originality, signaled them to wait for a moment. The big four-poster bed interested him. At a glance it was evident that it was a perfect example of the art of—but no! it had no particular style, it was unclassifiable.

This mass of carvings of unequal excellence, these motifs, so curious and unusual. An intuition flashed through the head of the decorator; he remembered the legends that clung around certain princely beds of the Renaissance, veritable secret chambers in themselves, in which stores of weapons or poisons were concealed, or which contained huge strong-boxes for the reception of money.

The decorator, to the astonishment of his colleagues, began to feel every carving, every sculptured motif. As he had the air of examining it solely from the standpoint of artistic taste, there were murmurs:

"We're losing time. Can't be anything here. Let's look somewhere else."

And in fact, if there were secret drawers, like those in the famous chamber of Catherine de Medicis at the Chateau de Blois, they were a long time in coming to light. The curious inquirer was about to abandon his task, when, suddenly, he felt something give under his fingers. At the same moment, behind the head of the bed, a large panel swung open in the wall, presenting to view a stairway large enough for three men to have mounted abreast. The movement had certainly lit an electric light somewhere, for the stairway was bathed in its glow.

The decorator was triumphant. But where did the stairway lead?

The group divided into three parts; the first was given the duty of climbing the stair; the second that of going down it, for it led down as well as up; the third remained in position.

Meanwhile, the visits to the rest of the house went on without incident. One group arrived at the garage and found it locked. The key was asked for in vain from the porter and the other servants; all declared that the Marquis usually carried it on his person. They added that there was a second key, but that the Chinese chauffeur always kept it.

The inquisitioners were not long in coming to a decision. They would break in the door.

Here, a remark is necessary. Crowds, like individuals, are capable of the most contradictory actions. Among those who burst into the Marquis' mansion were people of all classes and all types of morality. If some of them had arms on them, they never thought of using them. And others, whose morality had not always been of the highest character, thus participating in an act of public policy, never thought of committing the slightest theft.

They were incapable of stealing anything; but at the least sign of resistance, or the first suspicion, they were capable of destroying everything.

The garage door gave way at the first push. And the pushers halted suddenly, with the same exclamation of surprise as their companions on the second floor, at the sight of another secret stairway.

And, at the precise moment when the garage door gave way, a powerful touring car, all its lights ablaze, clashed suddenly into gear and charged away from them, directly at the rear wall of the garage!

Who was within? Who, rather than let himself be taken alive, was willing to dash himself and his car against the wall of the garage?

To the general stupefaction of all, the wall opened and then closed behind the auto as though it were made of gauze. The disappearance took place so swiftly that it seemed altogether unreal. A cry of rage swelled up behind the first cry of surprise.

"The brigand! He was in it! He's getting away!"

"Not for long. You can't lose an auto."

"Not when you have the number. But we haven't."

"Gentlemen," said the chief of the searching party, "we must continue our hunt."

Everyone was afire to discover the secret of the wall through which an automobile could pass. But this new incident, added to that of the bedroom when communicated to the group in the entry hall, and thence to the crowd in the streets, and so on its way through all

Paris, aroused the liveliest emotions. A little amplified, perhaps, even a little deformed in the telling, it arrived at the room where the ministers were still busily discussing the proper forms for an official inquiry into the Saint-Imier house.

It was decided to begin the inquiry without delay. But the machinery of justice is slow about getting in motion. And the responsible magistrates hesitated to issue the proper warrants, for they found no evidence of any reason for beginning official processes against anyone but the crowd who had invaded a private residence.

The crowd, meanwhile, was unembarrassed by these scruples. In the eyes of everyone present, the discoveries made so far justified pushing the search still further. That was why, instead of patiently looking for the opening in the rear wall of the garage, it was judged simpler to take it apart brick by brick, with chisel and pickaxe. In the twinkling of an eye, amateur house-wreckers were at work. They discovered immediately—and this did not surprise them—that the wall was nothing but a concealed partition, which contained neither bricks nor steel. A very ingenious system was quickly laid bare by the inexorable picks, by means of which the door was rolled back. Its ingenuity did not impress the observers; the only question they asked was:

"What are we going to find behind the wall?"

The reply was not long in coming. The wall once down, the searchers found themselves in another garage. And its doors were wide open on the Place de la Muette. The auto which had disappeared, with its lights ablaze, must be a long distance away by this time, on the Bois de Boulogne. The second garage contained two machines; another touring car and a low-bodied racer. Did they belong to the Marquis? Evidently not, for a guardian in livery appeared on the scene, at once angry and frightened, to protest against an intrusion, which in truth, could not be justified. But from questioner he was quickly turned into questioned. He must have known what had aroused the grumbling mob around him for he ceased his complaints, immediately, when he heard cries of: "We want to punish the baby killer!"

He was an individual with the olive skin of the typical South American, and he spoke with an accent:

"Gentlemen, I beg of you, don't hurt me."

"Good. But answer! Did you see an auto go out just now?"

"No, I swear to you. I was in the kitchen when I heard the noise of your pickaxes. It is for that I came out. But I saw nothing. I swear it!"

"Who owns this garage?"

"Señor Cuchillo."

"Ah, and where is Señor Cuchillo? We want to talk to him."

"Señor Cuchillo is in Biarritz."

A sly light appeared in the eyes of the guardian, but the crowd did not perceive the difference. Neighbors came to confirm the fact that house and garage did indeed belong to the rich Argentine.

The fact that the two garages were backed up to each other was not really abnormal. But another fact was at once curious and troubling; the two garages communicated with each other by means of a secret door, and the Marquis' auto had left the door of the rich Señor open.

"Bah!" said someone. "The police will clear that matter up. Let's go back to the Marquis' garage and see what other surprises we can find."

As a matter of fact, what was needed was a complete search, carried on, as rapidly as possible, to surprise the enemy in action if possible. A second sooner and they would have had the auto. Therefore speed was essential.

And as the search-party returned to the first garage, they seemed to hear behind the wall forming an angle with the demolished partition, footsteps and the sound of voices. Was this wall too, a fake? In any case, there came the sound of blows.

"Pickaxes up!"

The demolishers had already seized their tools and were preparing to tear down this second partition, when it opened suddenly—like that in the bedroom, and like that which had let the auto pass.

"It's us!" cried a voice. "Don't strike."

The picks fell to earth again. The new arrivals were part of the party which had been searching the upper floor, and who had gone down the secret stair to find out where it led to.

So, the secret stair led to the garage.

Therefore the Marquis could come in and go out without anyone in his house knowing about it, by using his private stairway and the Cuchillo garage.

The inquest was advancing—but without any direct proof of culpability. But had the garage delivered up all its secrets?

Before going back to the vestibule to report to the party in charge, the searchers resolved to make an inventory of everything in the garage. But as they began a terrific clamor came from the upper floor, spread abroad to the vestibule and the Court, and they left their task to run after the new discovery. There was a tempest, a hurricane of imprecations, a collective fury carried to the last limits, a release of one of those popular passions which nothing is capable of resisting. Fists were clenched, voices went high and hoarse, broken sentences were shouted.

"Death to the assassin! Lynch him! Death! Lynch him!"

What had happened?

The party that had gone to the secret stair had stepped on a landing corresponding to the third floor. The Marquis had been so certain that he would never be discovered that he had not even taken the precaution of turning the key in the door on this landing. The searchers penetrated into a huge bedroom, furnished with that elegant sense of luxury which is found only in the highest circles. The room had no lights but interior ones, no issue but a small skylight heavily barred. And it contained nothing but furniture.

But the searchers went on, certain that they would find something. There was another flight of stairs; they climbed to the fourth story, and penetrated into another room which opened on the hidden stairway; and here they gave an exclamation of triumph. For this was, without the slightest doubt, Saint-Imier's secret laboratory.

The first things to draw their attention were two huge mirrors, one concave, the other convex, mounted on universal joints which permitted them to be turned in any direction. Then the trituration tubes, the retorts, the glassware of the ordinary chemist; an electric furnace of extraordinary design and great power; a series of radioactive compounds in tubes; a radio receiving apparatus which at a first glance seemed like commercial apparatus, but in which certain details were peculiar, as for instance, the presence of two brilliant discs on the lateral faces; other machines, invented and made, certainly, by no other hands than those of the Marquis, whose use could only be told with certainty by experts, but which did not at first draw the attention of the searchers, and beyond, a doorway, leading to a private office.

On the table, papers were spread out. They were examined, at first cursorily; what interest or importance could scraps, of paper covered with figures, mathematical signs and hieroglyphical formulas have? But one of them was easier to read.

"Look, names and addresses. And figures. The Marquis' list of creditors with what he owes them."

There would have been a laugh at this pleasantry, had not one of the searchers cried:

"But that's the list of the dead children!"

CHAPTER XIX
THE DUPLICATE ASSASSIN

Every eye was directed at the tragic paper. The truth was as clear as day. On the scrap of paper, the Marquis had written the names of the children who had been struck down. And the list was too old to have been made after the crime.

Ten names, with the corresponding addresses were written in ink. Nine were struck out in pencil. The only name not crossed out was that of the child who had escaped, living in the Rue Duphot. And between the lines were written in pencil, the names of nine more children.

Opposite every name there were figures. What did they mean? Never mind, that could be discovered later—the important thing was that the proof was found at last. But the angry crowd need not worry now; they were certain of their game.

More pieces of paper were discovered. They were carefully classified. The first bore the heading: *Tomorrow evening, at 5*, and contained a list of 20 names. The second was headed: *Day after tomorrow, at 4*, and it contained 40 names. They corresponded exactly to the frightful program announced by the loudspeakers. The third scrap of paper was a sketch map of the streets at the east of the Halles Centrales. A semicircle, traced in blue crayon was around a section of it, and there were 20 points indicated in red crayon accompanied by mysterious numberings. A fourth slip of paper bore a similar sketch of the Montmartre district with 40 similar numbers and indicated points.

Thus, in the silence of his room, believing himself hidden from all eyes, disposing of forces against which there was no defense, this man had studied, in cold blood, and prepared the way for, the assassination of the population of a capital.

In the explosion of anger provoked by the discovery of these documents, one detail was not perceived; the secret stair led to the fifth floor and the room of the Chinese chauffeur, Pou-Hi. When it was finally discovered, the odor of the cigarettes the Chinese smoked habitually was still in the room; Pou-Hi had evidently left only a short time before. Further on a door communicated with the room of Suzie la Bretonne, and on the bed was a headdress in the style of Saint-Guénolé, newly pressed. It was therefore natural to conclude that the two servants were accomplices of their master. They, alone, could know of the existence of the stairway.

Moreover, everyone noticed that the lists of the persons the Marquis meant to slay bore their names, their first names and their ages. How had he been able to get such precise information and why? Would it not have been simpler to strike by chance?

Such questions the crowd relegated to the rear. What everyone wished was the immediate punishment of the criminal. And while waiting for that why not destroy his instruments? Yes, break everything in the laboratory. What did it matter what might still be discovered? The terrible pieces of paper were enough. The importance of a decisive proof is not helped by secondary proofs, no matter how good. As to giving the criminal to the ordinary processes of justice, what use would it be? No—violence was the only remedy.

Who gave the signal for the beginning of the destruction? Nobody. One would have said that everyone gave it at once. The sack of the laboratory began at the moment when the police, impotent against the gigantic crowd, appeared on the scene.

At the Elysée, the council of ministers was over. The President of the Republic, alone in his room, was reflecting on the grave events of the day. He had been kept advised, in some measure, of what was happening in the Rue Cortambert. The President's decision was made; the Marquis de Saint-Imier had escaped and it might not be easy to capture him. A call to arms of the whole country might be necessary. It was necessary to proclaim the Marquis a public outlaw.

All at once the telephone sounded. The features of the President expressed delight and surprise as he heard the voice of the Prefect of Police. The Paris police are ideally the best in the world! The Prefect announced that one of his inspectors had discovered the Marquis at the cabaret of the Cercle des Arts. He was taken immediately before an Investigating Magistrate. The Prefect added that all necessary precautions had been taken to prevent an escape. Delighted with this news, whose effect would be immense, the President hung up the receiver. But he was immediately recalled to the instrument. This time it was the Director of the secret police who wished to speak to the President in person. And the President in person gave signs of stifling when he heard the news:

"What? You say, my dear Director, that three of your inspectors have just arrested the Marquis de Saint-Imier? At the Cercle des Arts? What, what? They arrested him as he left the Princesse de Lezigny's house? Rue de Varenne? Are you certain? No resistance, hmm? They have taken him before an Investigating Magistrate. Well, tell me the news. I am curious to know the results of the questioning. Yes, thanks. Goodbye, my dear Director."

The President forgot to congratulate the zealous official who had thus transmitted a piece of news of the first importance, and who thought himself entitled to at least the ribbon of the Legion of Honor.

But the President, perplexed and troubled, suspected an unforeseen complication, also of the first importance.

How in the world could the same individual have been arrested in two spots widely separated from one another? How had the inspectors of the police department been able to meet the Marquis de Saint-Imier at the Cercle des Arts, two steps from the Etoile while the inspectors of the secret police were arresting him in the Rue de Varenne? Someone had lied or been deceived.

The President sighed. He knew the vagaries of public opinion. He knew that the Parisians have always been delighted by those good stories which permit them to laugh at government officials. That the frightful drama of the Rue Cortambert should become a means of laughing the government out of office, even before it reached its conclusion, was a little shocking. Something must be done to evade it.

But which one, the prefect or the director, had been deceived? And suddenly, the President thought:

What if neither of them had been deceived? With a man of Saint-Imier's type, anything can happen. I'm going to call the Ministry of the Interior.

He did not have time. The Minister of the Interior called him first, on a question of importance. The Saint-Imier mansion was in flames.

The arrest of the Marquis de Saint-Imier at the Cercle des Arts had not been attended by the slightest difficulty. The captain of police for the Muette quarter knew the Marquis very well and was on familiar terms with him. Saint-Imier affected to live in what he was pleased to call a "glass house." He took no kind of precautions, apparently, in his private life. Everybody seemed to know him. The papers took notice of his appearance at all the official solemnities, at all the notable receptions, the leading sporting events and society weddings.

Thus it was, that everyone knew that the Marquis had the habit of stopping in daily at the Cercle des Arts. A couple of good man-hunters, had been posted there without any great hope of finding their game, for nobody imagined that the game, so clearly unmasked, would have the impudence, or the imprudence, to come to his usual haunts.

Nevertheless, he came. He came late, but he came, and his lateness was only another reason for supposing, that at the time of his usual visit, he had been committing a crime. The Marquis had not even thought to provide himself with an alibi.

At the Cercle a half-dozen regular habitués were on hand, no more. These few were chatting about the wonderful progress being made in radio, which permitted a single individual to mystify all Paris.

The Marquis agreed with them, and added with indignation, somewhat surprising in a skeptic, that the police ought not to permit that sort of thing. Then, with a volubility not quite usual in a personage ordinarily reserved, he had expanded on the way in which crowds will believe anything at all. His six auditors remarked that he spoke rapidly, and without replying to remarks made by the others, as though he did not hear their questions, or rather, stared off into the distance as he spoke, as though unaware of their presence.

After which, he rose, passed into the reading room, ran briefly over the evening papers, which bore scare heads:

TEN CHILDREN KILLED BY UNKNOWN RADIATION
Police Search for Criminal

A copy of a later paper was handed to the Marquis by an employee of the establishment. He read aloud in a monotonous voice, and as though bored to death:

MOB ATTACKS ST.-IMIER HOUSE
Mysterious Auto Escapes Through Garage Wall

One would have expected him to be a little more stirred by this news. But he showed no sign of it if he were. He refolded the paper, put it in its rack, and with his monocle in his eye, stepped out into the hall of the Cercle, where he was pounced upon by four policemen, their revolvers in their hands, for they expected a furious resistance. But there was no resistance at all. The Marquis only asked, with a smile on his lips:

"*Sapristi!* What haste! What would you like, gentlemen?"

"You are Monsieur le Marquis de Saint-Imier?"

"Yes, but I regret to say I do not know you."

"We are police inspectors and we have a warrant for your arrest."

"That's odd," said the Marquis calmly, and then added:

"I am arrested then. Would you mind telling me what I ought to do? It's not usual for me, you understand. I have never been arrested before, but once, and then it was by a fog while I was flying over the North Pole."

The scoundrel dared to joke. An automobile drew up in answer to the policeman's signal.

"Get in quick," advised the inspector, "if you don't want to be lynched in the street."

The Marquis got in docilely beside his guardians. The position he was in seemed to leave him altogether unaffected. The auto went to the Palais de Justice, where Monsieur Blondel, the Magistrate in charge of the investigation, was to question him.

The other arrest of the Marquis took place almost simultaneously in the Rue de Varenne, and was due to a happy accident. Opposite the residence of the Princesse de Lezigny was a little wine merchant's shop. From time to time inspectors of the secret police came there to take a glass or two of *mousseux*. Now one of these, remembering having seen the Marquis' auto frequently halted before the Lezigny's, and knowing that Monsieur de Saint-Imier was usually to be seen at society receptions, placed himself on guard at the bar. He had the delight of hearing the wine merchant say:

"Ah, there comes the Marquis. He hasn't Pou-Hi with him today."

"Who is Pou-Hi?" asked the inspector.

"His chauffeur, of course. The Chinese."

"Ah, yes. True. The Marquis is driving himself."

It was the little car which the porter at the Saint-Imier mansion had mentioned to the invaders.

The inspector saw the Marquis go in, and telephoned for reinforcements.

About the same time, the Marquis, entering, perceived that he was alone in the salon.

"Ah," murmured Madame de Lezigny, "it's so good of you to have come. Do you know, I am dying of fear? Did you hear the radio?"

"Oh, yes, and I agree that it made a very disagreeable noise. Just the same, I see nothing to be frightened about."

"What, don't you know then—?"

"Oh, I never know anything. What happened?"

"The threats have been realized," said the princess, in a low voice, which seemed to be trembling with genuine fear.

The Marquis started:

"What do you mean?" he said.

"I just heard that ten children have died, as the loudspeakers predicted."

"But it's frightful."

"Isn't it? I don't dare to move any more. I hardly dare to breathe. It's frightful, Marquis, frightful."

"And incredible," said the Marquis. "Are you certain?"

"My brother just telephoned me about it. He said they were holding a ministerial council about it."

Monsieur de Saint-Imier could no longer doubt that the news was true. Madame de Lezigny's brother was an ambassadorial secretary attached to the foreign ministry, and would know at first hand.

The Princess went on:

"My brother told me I ought to join him. But I didn't dare to go out alone."

"Would you like me to accompany you as far as the Quai d'Orsay?"

"I would like it very much. With you, there would be nothing to fear."

The Marquis bowed.

On the sidewalk, as he bent to open the door of his car to show the princess in, he was rapidly surrounded by the vigorous agents of the secret police, while the head of the detachment made his excuses to the Princesse de Lezigny, explaining to her that he had a warrant to bring the Marquis de Saint-Imier in for questioning.

Fixing his monocle in his eye the latter turned to the princess:

"I am overwhelmed with regret at not being able to accompany you," he said with a smile. "But you see, what these gentlemen ask is impossible to refuse. I must go with them. Farewell, Madame."

He saluted with the grace of a gentleman and mounted into his own car between two of the detectives while a third took his place in the rumble-seat.

Ten minutes later, the Princesse de Lezigny was recounting this incredible story to her brother—to wit, that the most elegant man in Paris and perhaps in the world, had just been arrested. The Director of the secret police must certainly be crazy.

When she learned the truth, she had not even the strength to be surprised; she fainted with terror. She had been alone with the assassin for some minutes. She had placed herself under the care of the monster to drive about Paris. The story spread rapidly, and as soon as the unfortunate princess recovered from her faint, she was surrounded by an army of reporters, all of them wanting interviews with the woman who had seen the bandit arrested.

But the journalists, who had been prevented by the fire in the Saint-Imier mansion from visiting the secret stairway, the laboratory and the bedroom with its curious decorations, did not get all they hoped for.

In the first place, to avoid the popular tumult, the arrest of the Marquis was not officially announced until late at night. And the reporters could not know of the strange scene, the absolutely incredible scene that took place before the examining magistrate.

Monsieur Blondel was preparing to interrogate the Marquis de Saint-Imier arrested at the Cercle des Arts, when the Marquis de Saint-Imier arrested in the Rue de Varenne was brought in.

Very much astonished, the honorable Magistrate said to himself that one of the two was obviously not the man wanted. Which? It ought not to be too difficult to find out. Some of the policemen had made a mistake; that sort of thing happens every day. When they were confronted with each other, the unfortunate individual who had the bad luck to resemble the Marquis would be sent on his way, and the blunder of the police would be made good as soon as discovered.

But when Monsieur Blondel summoned the two, and saw before him two identical Marquis de Saint-Imiers, his stupefaction passed all bounds. He looked at his bailiff, who as astonished as he, stood by with his mouth open. Never, within the memory o the Msagistrate, had two accused persons resembled each other so much as this pair. Physically, the resemblance was absolutely perfect. And what finally upset the Magistrate was the fact that the two were dressed in exactly the same manner. Everything, even in the smallest details, was repeated.

"My word!" said Monsieur Blondel, rendered severe by his doubts, "has this been arranged in advance? But—but—they are absolutely interchangeable."

And the Magistrate, leaning over to the bailiff, whispered an order. Immediately, two athletic policemen placed themselves one behind each of the duplicate Marquis.

But the Magistrate reassured himself with the thought that the false one would certainly not wish to be confounded with the genuine.

CHAPTER XX
ESCAPE!

It was a delightful illusion. The two Marquis, identical in face and in costume, were also identical in their attitudes. The first Saint-Imier seated himself calmly in the chair that was placed for him; the second Saint-Imier, in the same 100th of a second, did the same. With the same gesture, they adjusted their monocles in their eyes; together they crossed their right legs over their left, and waited, the same ironic smile on both visages.

Monsieur Blondel had recovered his equilibrium. He threw a glance at the bailiff which signified:

"Patience! They'll come to their oats."

And he proceeded to the questions of identity.

It was dumbfounding. The two Marquis replied at the same time, articulating exactly the same words in the same voice, with the same intonations so exactly timed that one would have said it was a single voice that answered.

Monsieur Blondel wiggled his heavy eyebrows, and turning to the one on his right, he said dryly:

"You ought to understand, both of you, that it is not to your interest to perform such tricks before the bar of justice. The charges against one of you are exceptionally grave. I must recall to you that these questions of identity are for the purpose of distinguishing the innocent from the guilty person."

The facts were self-evident. Since it was impossible that there were two copies of the Marquis de Saint-Imier, it must be that one of the two before the Magistrate was a joke of a too original character abusing his incredible resemblance to the true Marquis. Saint-Imier's double was amusing himself? Well, he would not amuse himself for long. He risked having to pay a high price for his fun.

Monsieur Blondel went on:

"I address myself to you at my right. Are you the Marquis Guy-Gontran de Saint-Imier?"

The two Marquis inclined their heads with the same movement, and replied in unison:

"I am the Marquis Guy-Gontran de Saint-Imier, living at the Rue Cortambert, Paris."

"But I said nothing to you!" cried the Magistrate to the Marquis on his left. "Your turn will come, be quiet. It's not worth the trouble to tell me, both at once, that you are the Marquis de Saint-Imier. The Marquis de Saint-Imier is in danger of losing his head."

These words should have shot fear into the hearts of the two mummers. They replied only by the same smile of ironic appreciation. Monsieur Blondel, who had expected to interrogate the two together, before bringing in the evidence against one of them, was disconcerted for the moment.

Was he dealing with a pair of accomplices? But in that case, what was their game?

He repeated his question to the prisoner at the left:

"Do you declare that you are the Marquis de Saint-Imier?"

The two voices replied as one:

"I declare that I am the Marquis de Saint-Imier."

Monsieur Blondel was tempted to have the guards take away one of the two. But he gave over the idea, persuaded that the extravaganza could not be of long duration. Two individuals claimed the same personality they would therefore be subject to the same punishment, and let them beware!

And the Magistrate put a question that should end the difficulty:

"Where were you arrested?"

The two Marquises made together this stupefying response:

"I was arrested first in the Cercle des Arts in the Rue Presbourg, and then in the Rue de Varenne, in front of the Lezigny home."

This was really too much. What—the two individuals before the Magistrate pretended to be a single person? Evidently, the pretence could not be sustained. Nevertheless, they acted, they spoke as though the pretence were a reality. Moreover, they had the air of being ignorant of each other's existence; the Magistrate noticed that they never looked at each other. But the synchronization of their replies, made in the same words, with the same intonations of the voice, remained absolutely perfect. One would have said they were two automata, fabricated in series, and wound up so as to utter the same words.

Monsieur Blondel again addressed himself to the Marquis on his right:

"You were really arrested at the Cercle des Arts and again in the Rue de Varenne?"

"Yes," declared the two prisoners together.

The Magistrate lifted his head and said to the stenographer:

"Write down the double response."

"You are indeed the Marquis de Saint-Imier? And you, too, you are the Marquis de Saint-Imier?"

"I am the Marquis de Saint-Imier," repeated the two.

"In that case," pronounced the Magistrate, "for the first time in my life, I am going to give one order for two persons. Do you know of what you stand accused, gentlemen?"

The two Marquis lifted their heads, adjusted their monocles and replied in unison:

"Monsieur, do not give yourself the trouble to insist. I recognize the facts."

Monsieur Blondel could not restrain a movement of irritation:

"Be careful. The facts are of exceptional gravity. You cannot both be responsible. Look—you still have time to think it over between yourselves."

The two Marquis had the air of understanding no better than if Monsieur Blondel had spoken in Hebrew. Collective warnings decidedly were not going to have any effect. The Magistrate came back to the direct method, and this time, turned to the one on his left.

"You know, then, what it's about. Endangering the safety of the state; collective homicides…"

The two prisoners interrupted together:

"I know all that. Haven't I told you, Monsieur, that I recognize the facts?"

And in a tone of mockery, the two voices continued:

"You speak, Monsieur Blondel, of acts against the safety of the state. It is hardly sufficient. I wished to destroy, not the state, but the entire world. Not merely the world, but the universe. That is what I tried to do. The rest is only a detail. I suppressed two or three scoundrels who insulted me in the streets. I have also killed a few children—it's a detail, I repeat. Your laws are so stupid that this last act has become the principal accusation against me. It's enough to make one laugh. Monsieur

Blondel, if you please, consider me as the assassin of the whole human species. You will tell me that in fact, I have assassinated only a small part of it, and the intention does not make the fact.

"But, yes, I tell you. That which I have not yet realized, I will soon accomplish. You can thus consider that I am guilty, not of killing a score of humans but of millions, since I am going to make everything living disappear; then everything which contains the seeds of life. In a word, I admit all the charges that can be brought against me. I admit anything you wish. I declare that I regret nothing, and that I will complete my program. Will that do, Monsieur? Do I make myself clear? I am prepared to repeat these declarations to you if you have not understood them. But hurry up, for otherwise I will tell you nothing."

And the two prisoners made a slight bow in the direction of the judicial seat.

Monsieur Blondel was one of the most distinguished Investigating Magistrates of the Paris bench. He had handled numbers of celebrated cases. But never had he heard of a double personage charge himself with such audacity and such cynicism. As he heard the accusations the accused made against himself, he felt the hair on the back of his neck rise with terror. The two men before him were mocking justice. But they were no more than men. Their double comedy could not last much longer; the rude hand of justice had been placed on their shoulders, and justice would have the last word in this singular dialogue.

"They are held," he thought, and this thought helped his head cool; for a Magistrate must never lose his head. The Marquis and his companion were outraging justice—very well, justice would make them pay. Monsieur Blondel replied:

"I take cognizance of what you have told me, both of you. But I doubt, if you persist in that attitude, whether you will find a lawyer willing to defend you."

This unpleasant prospect did not seem to disquiet the two prisoners. Seated before the Magistrate, they kept their easy and impertinent calm, which they had kept since the beginning of the questioning. They never looked round at the guards placed behind them. The bailiff did not seem to exist for them. Nevertheless, when the judge announced that the record of their declarations was about to be read, they answered, always in perfect unison:

"Don't trouble yourself, Monsieur. But you may add that I declare this also—the people of Paris have sacked my mansion and set fire to it—"

Monsieur Blondel interrupted, stupefied:

"What? What are you saying?"

"The simple truth. The mob has set fire to my house."

"But how did you know that, since you left before the crowd arrived, and have not returned to see the spectacle of its just indignation?"

The Magistrate's question brought no reply. The two Marquis went on:

"I could complain of a crime committed against me also. Well, I do not complain. The imbeciles who believe they have disarmed me will soon discover that they have not limited my activities in the least, and I will now be pitiless: Paris will be destroyed! Every Parisian will be destroyed; not one will remain alive. But, you may be certain, Monsieur le Juge, that I will act correctly. Before striking, I will warn my victims. These victims will believe they will have time to escape. They will be very much surprised to find themselves unable to move. Yes, everyone will have time to fly, but no one will be able to. Don't you find the situation a bit comic, Monsieur Blondel?"

And the two sinister personages, in the presence of the Magistrate, the bailiff, the stenographer and the guards, began to laugh:

"Enough of this cynicism!" declared Monsieur Blondel, with a voice of thunder. "Stenographer, give the declarations to the prisoners to sign. Committed for trial!"

The stenographer had the impression that they would refuse to sign, on the usual pretext of prisoners who are interrogated without their lawyers being present. But the legal formalities must be observed, even with monsters, and he half rose to hand the pen to the nearest of the pair.

He fell back into his seat with a cry of astonishment and terror which was echoed by the Magistrate and the guards.

The two Marquis had disappeared! But their laughter was still vibrating through the room, and neither window nor door had been opened.

It was necessary to admit the fact; the two Marquis had escaped and the escape had been effected in a split second.

CHAPTER XXI
MAZELIER SACRIFICES HIS BEARD

The escape—or if one wishes, the double escape—of the Marquis de Saint-Imier, was not printed in the papers. The public supposed that the fantastic and redoubtable individual was under lock and key awaiting the inevitable hour of punishment. Nobody was surprised at the slow course of justice; everyone knew that she goes with one foot lame, especially when the Magistrates have so many mysteries to solve. But everyone was certain now; he, who had so audaciously announced his intentions over the loudspeakers, the noble who was now known under the name of *Radio-Terror*, was awaiting his punishment.

The greatest tranquility reigned in Paris. Thanks to Mazelier, normal life went on once more; the barrier of invisible radiation had been lifted from the capital and from the frontiers; there remained of the whole fantastic affair only the memory of an immense upheaval. And no one suspected the really decisive role that Mazelier had played in the solution of the problem. Already the story of the blockade was half forgotten. But, what no one did forget, what aroused the indignation of everyone when he thought about it, was the silent and cowardly assassination of the nine children. But now, thanks to the outburst of an angry people, all danger seemed over.

Three or four days after the burning of the Saint-Imier mansion, the newspapers contained the following note:

A terrible accident, which has provoked a consider-
able stir in scientific circles, occurred three or four days
ago at the Office for Scientific Research, Avenue des
Champs-Elysées. Monsieur Gribal, the distinguished
collaborator of the director of the office, Professor Ma-
zelier, was electrocuted in the course of an experiment.
There have already been several accidents of this cha-
racter, particularly in the field of radio-therapy, and this
makes only one more martyr to that science.

Professor Mazelier, himself, was gravely injured in
an explosion following the accident. His laboratory was
wrecked. With Monsieur Gribal's assistance, he was
engaged in studying the forms of radiation which
brought about the blockade of Paris and of the borders.
The distinguished scientist has been replaced as director
by the well-known chemist, Monsieur Reynier-Vitral.

In a little house hidden away in the bois of Ville
d'Avray, two men were reading this note, and one of
them was laughing.

"Well, I'm dead now, my dear Professor. You have
already resuscitated me twice, but I wasn't officially
killed then. How are you going to bring me back this
time?"

"Patience, Gribal! The moment has not yet come to
show ourselves in Paris. It is absolutely necessary that he
think we are out of the way."

"*Parbleu!* Do you think he will dare to continue the
combat?"

"I don't think it; I am certain of it. The man who
was able to escape in that strange manner from the Investigating Magistrate will never be wholly disarmed."

"All right. But he must be a little worried. And he
knows very well they are looking for him without offi-

cially announcing the fact. His photograph is everywhere."

"Yes. And he is nowhere. It bothers me that he doesn't come out."

"He's hiding."

"No, preparing for a new attack."

"But his laboratory is destroyed. What can he do without his apparatus. Nothing!"

"I hope so. Meanwhile, let's be on our guard."

"All right, my dear Professor. We'll watch. But I assure you that I do not partake of your fears. And the proof that I am right is that Roland never brings us the slightest bit of news. I assure you, I think we have gotten rid of that titled scoundrel for good. He has all Paris against him."

"We can wait, Gribal. But be careful."

"I will be. Just the same I would like to walk about Paris."

"I forbid you."

"And I will obey. What can I do anyway—I'm dead. It annoys me a little that no one has noticed I have had no funeral."

"You can be sure that *he* has noticed it."

"Oh, come. He can't do everything. He doesn't know everything. He's only a man, after all."

Mazelier lowered his voice:

"Listen, Gribal. There are certain moments when I doubt even that. Look—remember the circumstances of that double arrest. Those two doubles before the Magistrate. If the fact were not certified to me by the President of the Republic, I wouldn't believe it."

"And I," said Gribal, "I don't believe it yet! Well, since you wish it, we will wait."

The wait was prolonged for a month more. Roland Duplay, who could not be known to Saint-Imier, was the news-agent between Mazelier and the Elysée. Every evening, he came to Ville d'Avray, and every evening, he came without any news of importance. He was also given the duty of watching discreetly over the residence of Madame Roberval in the Rue Godot de Mauroy. This watch also yielded nothing. The Marquis had apparently ceased to hate the woman he had never ceased loving.

But one day Roland came earlier than usual, bearing strange news, but news not at all well verified.

A servitor of the Ministry of the Interior swore that he had seen the Marquis in the very office of the minister. Two members of the Cercle des Arts declared that they had seen him on the same day, at the same time, appear in the foyer of the opera house to disappear again immediately.

Gribal heard the news with a laugh:

"*Parbleu!*" he said. "It's not ordinary at least; a collective hallucination. You will hear tomorrow that the Marquis has been seen in Rome, in Chicago, at Timbuktu, and at the South Pole. And always at the same time."

"But," interrupted Roland timidly, "I think I saw him myself. Not at the same time but about two hours later."

"What, you too, Duplay? I should have thought you immune to such delusions."

Mazelier asked the young man:

"Where did you see him?"

"Rue Godot-de-Mauroy, 20 yards away from Madame Roberval's house. I assure you I was wide awake."

It was evident that Mazelier did not partake of Gribal's skepticism. On the contrary, he gave decided attention to the words of the young workman.

"And this…this vision, did it last long?"

"Not more than a couple of minutes."

"The Marquis went away. In what direction?"

"Monsieur, he didn't go away. He simply disappeared."

Mazelier did not laugh. Gribal became impatient.

"Oh, we can't discuss manifest impossibilities," he said. "Come, Professor, we—"

Mazelier interrupted:

"I think, Gribal, that I have never been able to see the limit which separates the possible from the impossible."

"Then you believe that several copies of the same individual can appear simultaneously in Paris?"

"I believe nothing, my friend. I deny nothing either. I think only of well-attested facts, whatever they may be."

Gribal was a man of good sense. It was difficult for him to admit anything but the most obvious explanations of a phenomenon.

"This fact," he said, "can be explained simply, in two ways. For example, if the Marquis has some accomplices who imitate his appearance and bearing, and if they show themselves in different places where he certainly is not present—"

"This hypothesis won't go, Gribal. The Marquis has no accomplices."

"What do you mean, no accomplices? He has at least two—the Chinese chauffeur, that's one—and that miserable Suzie. But there is another supposition equally reasonable."

"What is it?"

"That the Marquis' *Radio-Terror* has become a popular type like Cartouche and Fantômas. Jokers are amusing themselves by making up to resemble the Marquis de Saint-Imier, and startle people around them. There are always idiots who would think that sort of a masquerade funny."

Roland approved:

"It's possible," he admitted. "I thought of that, too."

Encouraged, and thinking he had now convinced Mazelier, Gribal continued:

"You speak of facts. Well, I'll give you another. Your revelator for radiation has been silent ever since they sacked the Marquis' mansion."

"Yes," admitted Mazelier, "nothing from that quarter since then. And my revelator is more powerful than it used to be. Saint-Imier cannot emit any forms of radiation without my hearing them now."

"Well, then? If the Marquis has not made a counter attack, it is because he has been reduced to powerlessness. Otherwise, as angry as he certainly must be, we would certainly hear from him. In consequence—"

"In consequence—?"

"*Parbleu!* I repeat it—we can go out and take the air and not stay shut up here. And that poor Madame Roberval, who remains shut up; won't you lighten her captivity? We are prisoners; it's simply ridiculous."

"You don't fear that the man who almost killed you will take the offensive again?"

"Not for a minute. He got his knock, that's enough to put some sense into his head."

"It should be, anyway. But it doesn't matter. Listen, Gribal, we must wait. And you, Roland, tell Madame Roberval from me, to be more careful than ever."

Gribal knew very well that Mazelier, once he had made his decision, would not alter it. Moreover, the scientist no longer heard his protests; he was sunk in a reverie so profound that he did not even notice when Paulette came in to ask the latest news from the Rue Boissy d'Anglas.

Three days went by like this, bringing no change in the situation of the voluntary prisoners. One afternoon, about 3 p.m., Mazelier and Gribal were at work in the laboratory where the scientist had installed his latest pieces of apparatus.

All at once the revelator began to vibrate.

"Oh, oh, it's waking up," cried Gribal, paling a trifle.

Mazelier was inspecting the movement of a needle across a dial and noting down figures.

Ten minutes later, another ringing from the revelator. No further doubt possible; the Marquis was neither disarmed nor inactive. He alone could have emitted the radiation which had stirred the revelator from its sleep. Mazelier and Gribal looked silently at each other, without the necessity of speech. What would Roland Duplay have to tell them?

He came in earlier than usual.

"Well, well?" questioned Gribal impatiently at his appearance.

"Nothing serious," replied the young man, surprised that his interlocutors already knew that something had happened. There was a little fire at Madame Roberval's, but they got it out quickly."

"At what time?" asked Mazelier.

"3:10 p.m. or thereabouts."

The engineer and the scientist exchanged glances.

"What caused the fire?"

"Nobody knows. It was queer. The fire started in her bedroom. A short circuit, they think."

"And at exactly 3 p.m.," Mazelier persisted, "didn't anything happen?"

"At 3 p.m.? No…Wait a minute, I forget. Something quite sensational did happen. But something that doesn't touch us at all. At 3 p.m., as the Minister of the Interior rose in the Chamber to make a speech, he fell dead."

Gribal was disconcerted:

"At 3 p.m.," he cried, "that must be it! But why should the Marquis wish to strike down the Minister of the Interior rather than anyone else?"

"What, Monsieur Gribal, was that death the work of the Marquis?"

But it was Mazelier who replied to Roland:

"Yes, my boy. And if you wish to know why, remember that the Minister of the Interior is the man who is said to have led the cabinet to pursue the judicial inquiry against Saint-Imier. Do you remember, Gribal? It was the Minister of the Interior who said to his colleagues: 'If every other murderer only knew that a sure means to avoiding suspicion was to invite you to dinner!' He has just died for having made that smart remark."

"And we, Mazelier, what are we going to do about it?"

"We? I think we have waited long enough. We must get busy without losing a minute."

"What? Now that there is really danger, we are going to go out?"

"Exactly. The moment has come. Roland and I, we will go into Paris together in a few minutes. We will separate at the Gare Saint-Lazare. Roland will tell Ma-

214

dame Roberval that by tomorrow she will be at liberty to come and go as she pleases. Understood? Whatever happens to her, she is never to forget that she is really safe and that unseen protectors are watching over her. Right?"

"Right, Professor Mazelier."

"Then, Roland, you will meet me again about 8 p.m. in front of No. 20, Rue Fabert. Ah, wait a minute...as you probably will not recognize me, I had better show myself to you as I will appear when I meet you there. I have already camouflaged myself once—not so, Gribal? And they picked me out right away. But this time! You will see. A moment, if you please."

Mazelier went into his room. 15 minutes later he came back, quite unrecognizable. He had cut his beard and curled his hair. No more and no less, but the change was extraordinary.

"Who disguises himself too much, does not disguise himself at all," he remarked with a laugh. "That's axiomatic. Don't I look like a retired mailman, Gribal? Well, Roland, come along. After meeting in the Rue Fabert, we will take a little walk toward Grenelle. And be sure to have a gun with you."

"And me?" asked Gribal. "Are you going to leave me shamefully inactive?"

"You, my dear friend, you are dead. Don't forget it. There's nothing more compromising than to go for a walk in Grenelle with a dead man! And besides, you can't change your face as easily as I can. Tel me, am I ugly enough?"

The fact was that Mazelier, without his little beard and corona of white hair, was far removed from manly beauty.

Gribal resigned himself to inaction with a bad grace. He had to give in, however, without understanding the hazardous project on which his superior was engaged.

CHAPTER XXII
TRIPLEX

Ghislaine Roberval had attached no particular importance to the minor fire in her bedroom. She received with an inexpressible sense of relief the message from Mazelier. Yes, beginning the following morning she would go out to fulfill her duty of placing new flowers by the tomb that held the remains of Gabriel de Neuville.

The next morning, about 8 a.m., she called a taxi which was passing her door. To her great surprise, the chauffeur—he had doubtless misunderstood her directions—took the Rue Royale and went toward the Place de la Concorde. That was the wrong direction. She knocked on the window; the chauffeur half-turned. He had a singular face, yellow of tint, with a cruel mouth.

Where had Ghislaine seen that mask of a face before? All at once she remembered—the Chinese chauffeur! The familiar of Saint-Imier. She gave a cry of terror, and half rose to leap from the car, in spite of the speed with which it was going down the Rue de Bourgogne, when a voice seemed to murmur in her very ear:

"Don't be afraid! There is not the slightest danger."

She almost fainted with terror. The Marquis was seated by her side! Ghislaine tried to open the door at her side; she did not succeed; the door seemed to be locked solidly into the side of the machine. She reached for the door on the other side, and then fell back with an exclamation of terror. For her arm had passed through the body of the Marquis as though it were not there, as though it were nothing but a ghost. And the Marquis, his hands on his knees, remarked calmly:

"No danger, I assure you. You will understand that I have taken every precaution."

The precautions signified that any attempt at escape would be futile. Trembling, Ghislaine sank back in the corner of the car, and then recalled, suddenly, the message from Mazelier: "No matter what happens, unseen watchers will guard you."

But how had she been so easily trapped?

Tearing along, as though it were running a race, the auto did not stop till it reached the Rue Javel, where it pulled up before a sordid-looking building. The Marquis got out first, and with his characteristic politeness, removing his hat, said:

"Will you follow me, my dear? I would like to have you attend my house warming in my new home."

What audacity! Ghislaine leaped from the vehicle, resolved to fly down the street, to cry for aid, for there were some passers-by in view.

But she neither cried nor fled; she followed her captor, trembling, as though enchanted, dominated by some inexplicable force that rendered her as inert as the hands of a watch.

Saint-Imier, preceding Ghislaine, and by this sign, certain that she was following him, went up a dark and narrow stairway. Decidedly, his new house had not the elegance of the old. Nobody had apparently paid any attention to the strange couple. The Marquis marched gaily ahead with long steps; Ghislaine following as rapidly as she could not knowing by what miracle she was able to move limbs paralyzed with fright.

At the fifth floor, she felt a sudden return of her forces, and would have turned and fled; and then she turned back again with an exclamation of horror. The Marquis was behind her! She went up another step or two—the Marquis was before her. The two Saint-Imiers, who had already been seen by the Investigating Magistrate, had surrounded Ghislaine, and she, overcome with terror, was sure that nothing could save her. And the ironic voice of her double kidnaper announced:

"Don't hurry, my dear. We have all the time in the world. Besides, it's only two more flights to *our* apartment."

The terrible ascent went on. On the landing of the seventh floor, the trio halted. Ghislaine no longer dared to look at her captors. Finally, a narrow door opened and an African in livery, with a silkily polite voice, bowed before her:

"Enter, Madame. We are pleased to have the honor of your presence."

Ghislaine went in. She took several steps and found herself in a room only feebly lighted. Windows and blinds were closed tight. Suddenly, she perceived that she was alone. What had become of her two guardians? She did not have time to look for them; at the other end of the room a door opened, and the Marquis—a single Marquis—came in.

"Good afternoon, Ghislaine," he said, as though he had not seen her before. "Sit down, I beg you. Are you not a little astonished at what has been happening to you?"

She did not answer. First, because she did not wish to answer; and secondly, because she was trying to assemble her whirling thoughts. It seemed to her that the man who stood before her had a more sonorous voice, a more lively eye, than he—or those who had accompanied her. Yes, she might almost have said that the others were his reflections.

By no means disconcerted by the silence of his victim, and at ease as much as in the salons of which he was an ornament, Saint-Imier seated himself in an armchair beside a table surmounted by gleaming instruments.

"You permit?" he murmured and lit a cigarette. Then: "Listen, Ghislaine, I owe you an explanation. I will give it to you completely. You must have been astonished, in your taxi as well as on the stairway, to see me appear, and to redouble myself the better to escort you up the stairs. Here, look at this machine."

Ghislaine noticed on the table a sort of rectangular box, and emerging from the box an object which resembled a metal ball with a wire which ran round the outside of the container.

"Look," said the Marquis, "I close a contact here. I turn this button. Observe the lights that appear around the ball and the velocity with which it turns You don't understand what it is for? Well, it produces two more Marquis de Saint-Imiers, that's all. Oh, *Mon Dieu*, yes, it's perfectly true, as I have the honor of telling you. I am seated comfortably in my armchair. I put this apparatus in motion and two emanations, two projections of myself, are materialized. Isn't it practical for making calls you don't care to make in person?"

He laughed; and then a note of pride crept into his voice:

"Very convenient," he went on. "My projections go immediately to any spot where I want them to go; whatever anyone says to them, I hear it here; whatever is going on around them, I see; whatever I wish them to say, they say. In brief, they are two other selves which I can cause to appear and disappear as I wish. They have only this disadvantage, that both of them must act alike. Do you understand, Madame? In a few minutes, we will have a little experiment with them, with the object of amusing you, Madame."

The last words were pronounced with such an indefinable accent of cruelty that the blood seemed to freeze in the veins of the prisoner.

He laughed gently, exaggerated a trifle by his super polite air of a man of the world:

"If you permit, we will begin now. And you will see."

He approached his box, made a contact, turned a button and then another. The ball began to turn; colored balls of light appeared, surrounding it, gyrating in the opposite direction. A soft purring sound filled the room. And slowly, out of the whirling clouds of light, the two personifications of Saint-Imier appeared, immobile before him like two well-trained servants.

"Do you know where I am going to send them?" asked Saint-Imier, addressing himself to Ghislaine. "They are going into various well chosen localities in the world of society to tell a few little stories about you and your private life. We will start with that, my dear. They will add that you are in a sanitarium, recovering from the effects of your last excesses. And it was you, of course, who furnished me with the list of children destined to be killed."

"You scoundrel," cried Ghislaine.

"Oh, there will be lots of other touches, my dear. And in any case, with my two agents here who can penetrate any doors, and who can speak to anyone and be questioned by no one without my permission, I will be surprised if I do not finish by laying on your shoulders the responsibility for what has happened."

He turned the little lever.

The two phantoms did not move.

An exclamation of surprise escaped the Marquis. But he did not glance at the two reflections of himself which had risen before the astonished eyes of Ghislaine.

"What's wrong now?" he said aloud, bending over the opened box.

"I ought not to keep you in ignorance, Ghislaine. It was I who lit a little fire for you yesterday afternoon. If you hadn't gone out this morning, there would have been another. I was intending to smoke you out, do you see? Ah, yes, and another thing. I believe that about the same time, I damaged the Minister of the Interior who was so injudicious as to defend your interests a little too strongly against me. I gave him the same dose that Gabriel de Neuville got. You remember? Would you like me to show you how it's done? I can try it on some other subjects."

Ghislaine rose. The Marquis turned toward her.

"Ah, dear lady," he said, "we're really going to have a good time. You can't go out, you know, but you can do anything you like in here."

He threw the little lever again. The two phantoms moved no more than they had the first time. The Marquis cried, impatiently:

"This is annoying. There is certainly something wrong with this machine. Well, we'll hold over the little trip through the Paris salons for another day. I must return the emanations of my corporeal body to nothing."

He broke the contacts, an act which should have produced the immediate disappearance of the two. But instead of vanishing into thin air, they advanced a step toward the Marquis, and cried in a single voice:

"I am the Marquis de Saint-Imier!"

The genuine Marquis did not lose countenance. He remarked:

"Well, well, and now we have talking machines that express opinions, and in voices unlike their master's. It's queer to say the least."

The two reflections turned toward Ghislaine together.

"That woman is mine," they declared.

And they continued to advance toward Saint-Imier, who moved back a step.

"What a good idea!" he said. "That's it, Ghislaine, how would you like to belong to two Saint-Imiers?"

But the two apparitions, now become rebels to their creator, continued to advance without another glance at the young woman. The moment arrived when the Marquis found himself so pinched between his two doubles that it was only by physical effort that he could escape them.

In an instant the fantastic adventure became a drama. As though in a frightening dream Ghislaine found herself the spectator of a combat between the two copies of the man and the man himself. Three Saint-Imiers were fighting among themselves with an extraordinary violence. The Marquis was like a man fighting with his image in a mirror; every blow he struck was returned to him with double force; and nothing could be stranger than this triple combat in which two members acted exactly alike. Saint-Imier, his face showing his sudden fright at the discovery that the beings he had created, had, like himself, flesh and bones, essayed to seize one of them by the throat; but as he did so, his own throat was seized in a double grip and he fell at the feet of Ghislaine overwhelmed with horror.

Whether the death of the Marquis brought about the disappearance of his reflections or not, or what strange medley of projections and images had brought the thing to pass, Ghislaine did not know. She knew, only, that in an instant she was alone, and at her feet was the dead body of the *Radio-Terror*.

Alone? No, for the door through which the Marquis had come, opened again and through it appeared— Mazelier and Roland Duplay!

For the scientist had gained his greatest and final victory. Substituting, with more powerful radiation, his own control for that of the Marquis, he had directed the phantom figures against their creator, and, at bottom, the combat among the three Saint-Imiers had been not a combat but a suicide.

Before the corpse of the aristocratic and heartless scientist, Roland paused a moment to say:

"At last his victims are avenged!"

But Ghislaine added in a tone of sadness:

"Alas! Your vengeance does not give me back those I weep for."

Mazelier did not try to console her. Without a word he took her arm, and the three of them left without even another glance at the remains of the man, who, made mad by pride, thought of accomplishing everything by intelligence without the admixture of a generous heart and clean hands.

SF & FANTASY

Guy d'Armen. *Doc Ardan: The City of Gold and Lepers*
G.-J. Arnaud. *The Ice Company*
Cyprien Bérard. *The Vampire Lord Ruthwen*
Aloysius Bertrand. *Gaspard de la Nuit*
Richard Bessière. *The Gardens of the Apocalypse*
Félix Bodin. *The Novel of the Future*
André Caroff. *The Terror of Madame Atomos*
Didier de Chousy. *Ignis*
Captain Danrit. *Undersea Odyssey*
C. I. Defontenay. *Star (Psi Cassiopeia)*
Charles Derennes. *The People of the Pole*
Georges Dodds (anthologist). *The Missing Link*
Harry Dickson. *The Heir of Dracula*
Jules Dornay. *Lord Ruthven Begins*
Sâr Dubnotal *vs. Jack the Ripper*
Alexandre Dumas. *The Return of Lord Ruthven*
J.-C. Dunyach. *The Night Orchid; The Thieves of Silence*
Henri Duvernois. *The Man Who Found Himself*
Achille Eyraud. *Voyage to Venus*
Henri Falk. *The Age of Lead*
Paul Féval. *Anne of the Isles; Knightshade; Revenants; Vampire City;*
The Vampire Countess; The Wandering Jew's Daughter
Paul Féval, *fils. Felifax, the Tiger-Man*
Arnould Galopin. *Doctor Omega*
G.L. Gick. *Harry Dickson and the Werewolf of Rutherford Grange*
Nathalie Henneberg. *The Green Gods*
V. Hugo, P. Foucher & P. Meurice. *The Hunchback of Notre-Dame*
Michel Jeury. *Chronolysis*
Octave Joncquel & Theo Varlet. *The Martian Epic*
Gérard Klein. *The Mote in Time's Eye*
Jean de La Hire. *Enter the Nyctalope; The Nyctalope on Mars; The*
Nyctalope vs. Lucifer
André Laurie. *Spiridon*
Georges Le Faure & Henri de Graffigny. *The Extraordinary Adven-*
tures of a Russian Scientist Across the Solar System (2 vols.)
Gustave Le Rouge. *The Vampires of Mars*
Jules Lermina. *Mysteryville; Panic in Paris; To-Ho and the Gold*
Destroyers; The Secret of Zippelius
Jean-Marc & Randy Lofficier. *Edgar Allan Poe on Mars; The Katri-*
na Protocol; Pacifica; Robonocchio; Tales of the Shadowmen 1-7

Xavier Mauméjean. *The League of Heroes*
John-Antoine Nau. *Enemy Force*
Marie Nizet. *Captain Vampire*
C. Nodier, A. Beraud & Toussaint-Merle. *Frankenstein*
Henri de Parville. *An Inhabitant of the Planet Mars*
J. Polidori, C. Nodier, E. Scribe. *Lord Ruthven the Vampire*
P.-A. Ponson du Terrail. *The Vampire and the Devil's Son*
Maurice Renard. *The Blue Peril; Doctor Lerne; The Doctored Man; A Man Among the Microbes; The Master of Light*
Albert Robida. *The Adventures of Saturnin Farandoul; The Clock of the Centuries; Chalet in the Sky*
J.-H. Rosny Aîné. *Helgvor of the Blue River; The Givreuse Enigma; The Mysterious Force; The Navigators of Space; Vamireh; The World of the Variants; The Young Vampire*
Han Ryner. *The Superhumans*
Brian Stableford. *The New Faust at the Tragicomique; The Empire of the Necromancers (The Shadow of Frankenstein; Frankenstein and the Vampire Countess; Frankenstein in London); Sherlock Holmes & The Vampires of Eternity; The Stones of Camelot; The Wayward Muse.* (anthologist) *The Germans on Venus; News from the Moon; The Supreme Progress*
Jacques Spitz. *The Eye of Purgatory*
Kurt Steiner. *Ortog*
Eugène Thébault. *Radio-Terror*
Villiers de l'Isle-Adam. *The Scaffold; The Vampire Soul*
Philippe Ward. *Artahe*
Philippe Ward & Sylvie Miller. *The Song of Montségur*

MYSTERIES & THRILLERS

M. Allain & P. Souvestre. *The Daughter of Fantômas*
A. Anicet-Bourgeois, Lucien Dabril. *Rocambole*
A. Bisson & G. Livet. *Nick Carter vs. Fantômas*
V. Darlay & H. de Gorsse. *Lupin vs. Holmes: The Stage Play*
Paul Féval. *Gentlemen of the Night; John Devil; The Black Coats ('Salem Street; The Invisible Weapon; The Parisian Jungle; The Companions of the Treasure; Heart of Steel; The Cadet Gang)*
Emile Gaboriau. *Monsieur Lecoq*
Steve Leadley. *Sherlock Holmes: The Circle of Blood*
Maurice Leblanc. *Arsène Lupin vs. Countess Cagliostro; Lupin vs. Holmes (The Blonde Phantom; The Hollow Needle)*

Gaston Leroux. *Chéri-Bibi; The Phantom of the Opera; Rouletabille & the Mystery of the Yellow Room*
William Patrick Maynard. *The Terror of Fu Manchu*
Frank J. Morlock. *Sherlock Holmes: The Grand Horizontals*
P. de Wattyne & Y. Walter. *Sherlock Holmes vs. Fantômas*
David White. *Fantômas in America*

SCREENPLAYS

Mike Baron. *The Iron Triangle*
Emma Bull & Will Shetterly. *Nightspeeder; War for the Oaks*
Gerry Conway & Roy Thomas. *Doc Dynamo*
Steve Englehart. *Majorca*
James Hudnall. *The Devastator*
Jean-Marc & Randy Lofficier. *Royal Flush*
J.-M. & R. Lofficier & Marc Agapit. *Despair*
Andrew Paquette. *Peripheral Vision*
R. Thomas, J. Hendler & L. Sprague de Camp. *Rivers of Time*

NON-FICTION

Stephen R. Bissette. *Blur 1-5; Green Mountain Cinema 1; Teen Angels & New Mutants*
Win Scott Eckert. *Crossovers* (2 vols.)
Jean-Marc & Randy Lofficier. *Shadowmen* (2 vols.)
Randy Lofficier. *Over Here*

HEXAGON COMICS

Franco Frescura & Luciano Bernasconi. *Wampus*
Franco Frescura & Giorgio Trevisan. *CLASH*
L. Bernasconi, J.-M. Lofficier & Juan Roncagliolo Berger. *Phenix*
Claude Legrand, J.-M. Lofficier & L. Bernasconi. *Kabur*
Franco Oneta. *Zembla*
L. Buffolente, Lofficier & J.-J. Dzialowski. *Strangers: Homicron*
Danilo Grossi. *Strangers: Jaydee*
Claude Legrand & Luciano Bernasconi. *Strangers: Starlock*

ART BOOKS

Jean-Pierre Normand. *Science Fiction Illustrations*
Raven Okeefe. *Raven's L'il Critters*
Randy Lofficier & Raven OKeefe. *If Your Possum Go Daylight...*
Daniele Serra. *Illusions*